LEE

ALSO BY TITO PERDUE

Fields of Asphodel

LEE

A NOVEL BY TITO PERDUE

THE OVERLOOK PRESS
Woodstock & New York

This edition first published in the United States in 2007 by
The Overlook Press, Peter Mayer Publishers, Inc.
Woodstock & New York

WOODSTOCK:
One Overlook Drive
Woodstock, NY 12498
www.overlookpress.com
[for individual orders, bulk and special sales, contact our Woodstock office]

NEW YORK:
141 Wooster Street
New York, NY 10012

The epigraph by George Grote on the facing page refers to one of the Kings of ancient Sparta who went hopelessly insane in old age, from Grote's ten-volume history of Greece

Library of Congress Cataloging-in-Publication Data

Perdue, Tito.
Lee : a novel / by Tito Perdue.
p. cm.
I. Title.
PS3566.E691225L44 1991 813'.54—dc20 91-9477

Manufactured in the United States of America
ISBN-10 1-58567-872-4 / ISBN-13 978-1-58567-872-3
10 9 8 7 6 5 4 3 2 1

His habitual violence of character became aggravated into decided insanity, insomuch that he struck with his stick whomsoever he met.

—Grote

LEE

One

THERE WERE HILLS BEHIND HIM (smoke coming off the summits) and fields of a yellowness that made him moan out loud—so must have felt the first man, seeing he was alone upon the world. He could foretell all: billions upon billions of years in a place with seasons, and hills that were sometimes here and sometimes there, and billions more still until Time had had enough.

He liked to walk for perhaps an hour, with long stops between, and then to come upon a high place with a view of the rueful beauty of earth and all that had taken place upon it. Sometimes, it was good: a plot turning back to weed, a ruined barn with vertebrae sticking out. Watching closely, he would begin to piece together in imagination the love affair, notorious in its day, that had perhaps worked itself out where he was standing, and perhaps was working itself out still.

He pushed on. Lately, he had taken to using a stick that, with his satchel and tattered clothes, had a way of making dogs burst into song. His ankles were worn down to a thinness. Moreover, he looked excessively sly.

He knew what he knew, and it was this that kept him away from cities. Not that there were any great settlements along his route! On the contrary, he had been traveling all day amid nothing but ruined fields and barns. Now, in truth, he began to have that feeling the first man surely felt, namely, that it was his part to keep moving, that he was alone, that very probably the world with all its smoke and mountains extended on in perpetuity forever.

He had felt that same feeling seventy years ago; now, suddenly, he popped up over a hill and there it was. He had seen it before, this town. It pleased him that it was no larger than it was, that there had even, perhaps, been some erosion about the western edge where the poverty had dwelt. He spied a tumbledown house and, next to it, another, bending slowly to earth. Knowing what he knew, he could bring up an entire block and look it over in detail. But his desire was to plunge forward and begin at once reintroducing himself to everyone whom he had known. They might organize a celebration! No, they were dead, most of them (science said so), or at any rate old now beyond all recognition.

He waited for night. The town itself was green this hour, the same green shadows he remembered and same yellow moon (his own special star) with holes in it. Life seemed extinct, save for one grainy light in a window where someone, old no doubt, was even now sitting in a barren room and gazing into nothing. He did so love it, the method of night in small towns with history's survivors. And now he saw that which he had not seen in thirty years—a neon sign, sputtering and feeble and near to going out. He had *not* imagined it, there *had* been such an epoch. Moreover, he had been inside that very shop one time.

He heard the sound of his own footfall, something to muse upon. Ahead was a narrow building with a clock that looked down most ruefully upon one who had turned up again after so much time, dressed in the way that he was. He remembered there had been a bakery next door, but it was now turned into a realtor's office, around which, however, some of the divine odor seemed still to linger. In former times he used to fly down this hill on his bicycle, but now it seemed the merest rising, hardly enough to weary an old man on the upward climb.

In fact all things were smaller, less, more level, littler. Every decade of his life had seen the demise of something that once . . . And now he felt that he was a stranger on shore while the town itself had taken ship and was bobbing out to sea.

He turned, keeping one eye at all times on the display of paper-thin clouds and dangling moon. In this district the homes had high-peaked roofs of the kind he remembered, and one of them so old-fashioned that it had either a vane or actual cock posturing on the gable. He saw frosted windows from the Genteel Age. Lee halted. By his reckoning he was drawing near to the place, and yet he was reluctant to go up and check the address. Suddenly, he leapt—a train two miles away shrieked wretchedly with the sound that knows when it is the last of its species left on earth.

He spied a porch with a chest on it, and going up to it, he verified that the chest was his own. This house had three stories, not two, and a roof that was yet higher and steeper and more baleful than the others. This pleased him, as did the scent of new paint applied solicitously over rotted wood. First he set foot in the yard; then he ran around to the rear of the building in profound shadow. All these tenants were unconscious or dreaming; all lights were dimmed.

He returned to the front porch, took out an envelope and key, and tried the lock, which opened easily. His first impression was of an immense room, so large he could flail his arms around while striking nothing. He remained still, adapting to it, then he finally edged to the stairs that lay under deep carpet. His own room was on the top floor, and there was a corridor that tapered down so narrowly as to give him trouble with his bag. The apartment was his, paid for fully, and yet he found himself tapping politely lest he blunder in upon someone who might have set up happily in his absence. Instead, it was empty, empty and stark and with but a few odds and ends of old furniture that looked more of European origin than of this place where he was. Also, he saw a mirror, grayed and with a scum on it, showing the opposite wall.

Certainly it had some of the qualities of death—that of sitting in a strange new place, recently painted, where a long line of insignificant people had been dwelling before him. "One soul in two bodies," and now one was gone. It was for this that he must have at least two rooms—for saying that *she* was just around the corner.

Two

HE WOKE IN A SMEAR OF LIGHT; then, seeing that the ceiling was far above and unfamiliar, he forced himself down again. In the next apartment someone was speaking in a low, serious voice. Also, he heard the sound of a cup clashing in a saucer. He could not have said whether he were asleep or waking, only that the sun, which was orange and had spots on it, seemed trapped within the window frame.

He rose painfully and made a quick tour of the rooms, both of them quite bare. The mirror, the same that just hours ago had been deep and green, was now a mere bland sheet. He saw that the bureau was missing a leg. In its place stood a common jar with lid, which he marked down at once as a hiding place for small things. The other room had shelves in it, floor to ceiling in fact, space enough for the better part of his books, and this cheered him. Moreover, the view here looked down into the western district with its shacks and slum, while on the other side, he could see out for miles over a countryside in which, even as he watched, a long line of cattle was moving out to feed.

He shaved slowly, almost falling asleep at it. In younger days he had enjoyed dressing poorly for the effect of it, now he was grateful for any little remediation that clothing could bestow. He had a hat, yesterday's suit, also two good shoes in glossy condition. And he had money, the proceeds from sale of his last seventy-five acres. He liked a full wallet, liked to take two or three of the larger bills and hide them on his person where no one would dream to search.

It was fine weather outside, sweet with a blue sky. On the front porch the chest of books remained to be taken upstairs. He went two blocks, and the homes became more and more familiar to him. Only yesterday he had been traveling in the forest, now he was within inches of where he had spent his childhood. Suddenly, that moment, a tiny dog on vestigial legs, a sorry representative of a once-great race, came yapping asthmatically at him; Lee was shocked. In his day such a thing would have never dared to taunt a full-grown man of maturity and ask to go on surviving. He sought for a stone and found it, but then he opted not to stoop for it and have to fight his way back to standing position.

He saw the chimney first, and knew then the house existed still. His own room came into view, or rather the window where he used to spend so much time in nervous vigils. Formerly, there had been a mess of bicycles strewn on the porch, and often as not, his short brother would be standing palely in his baseball cap. Now, Lee could not be sure anyone lived there anymore.

He moved past, coming to a field that had been filled over and built with houses that were themselves getting old. People had been born, had lived and died, all in the time that he had been away.

Lee crossed the road and came back, allowing himself, as it were, to be pushed by the breeze and mild weather. He had to admit it: The place had been kept in good condition, perhaps in recognition that it had once housed someone who might almost have been famous. He felt himself softening toward all such small folk of this earth as spent their little time in mowing and sweeping and toddling off to work. Indeed he saw one now—a good man in a hat who, although it was the middle of the morning, had strayed away all unknowingly from home, office, or factory. Lee's first impulse was to report him to the authorities; his second, to stop and reveal himself as that same boy who used to rouse the neighborhood. Instead, he followed the man to the corner, and then, with the fellow glancing nervously behind, Lee followed all the way to the gate where Alice used to live. *Now* Lee knew what was missing—the children. Where were they? Inside, all of them, watching television.

He went on, pursuing the same road out of long-ago habit. In his day these had been places of interest, a twenty-acre slice of woods with tree houses and each with an inhabitant in it; now, from the expression on people's faces, he might almost have been up North. He passed a youth, cynical-looking, mouth hanging open in a kind of late twentieth-century stupor—he had seen this syndrome before, and now apparently it had spread to Alabama as well. His gorge was rising. Ahead (he almost hated to look inside) was a shop in which a certain merry woman used to sell comestibles. What he saw now was a haughty-looking girl in expensive clothes and jewelry, seated amid a computer array.

Main Street seemed the same, except that now it looked strangely hollowed out and had only a small amount of traffic. He passed a dress shop, in the window the same rapturous mannequin with spiritual face that he had once caught in the nude. The movie house had been turned into a furniture outlet that had long ago closed down and now was crumbling even as he watched. Before, he had thought it a long distance between this and the drugstore; now, he saw it was but a matter of steps. All things were smaller, all littler. But mostly it was the simplicity he regretted. The world was so much richer, the people so much more knowing, and yet every face he saw seemed coated with something, sleepiness perhaps, together with cases of outright corruption.

He had one eye upon his own shadow, so gaunt and elongated that it seemed already to belong to the literature of the past. It is true that he took pleasure in making himself as grim as possible. He wore black clothes and glasses that made his eyes goggle; he had sometimes seen people break off in midconversation when viewing him for the first time. At that moment, smiling to himself, he suddenly hit upon a shop that specialized in pipes and tobacco and that had a goodly selection of old-fashioned walking sticks on display. When he set eyes upon them, he couldn't imagine how he had come through so many years without such a thing for himself.

He should have known the proprietor would be old and irritable, and so it proved; they looked at each other in great annoyance. The sticks themselves were lined up on one side, a good choice, even if the better part of them were too delicate by far for any usages of his. What he *wanted* would be gnarled and heavy, stalwart enough for smashing skulls; what he *found* was a "cane," so-called, with a head on it. Suddenly, he pulled it out and began slashing wildly about, four or five times, before taking it over to the man who was watching in concern. Looking at him, Lee had the impression this person was stuffed with straw, as it were, and that instead of hair, the straw was running out at the top.

"Well. I suppose this will have to do." (Again, he swung wildly.) "Where can a person get some coffee around here?"

"Coffee? Why, there's any number of places."

"But I'm asking for the *nearest* place."

"There's lots of them too."

"Well I'll be goddamn, you're not going to say, is that it?"

They glared. The man had a defect, a tic, also an opening where some of the straw was sticking out.

"There's Perry's."

"Perry's."

"You'll see it."

Lee paid, taking one bill from his vest, letting the man get a good long look at it, and then getting the remainder from his puffy wallet. Outside it was warm. He went on, talking to himself, a full block before he realized he had come away without his "cane" and had to return for it.

He found Perry's nowhere, neither here nor on the other side of the road. Instead, a hundred yards on, he came to a restaurant of sorts with tables and umbrellas out front in the French style. There was a crowd of gesticulating sixteen- and seventeen-year-olds all talking at the same time—he wanted to puke. They simply could *not* sit still. All his life he had wanted to identify what it was the masses most loathed, and then to see that they got it in spades. What he craved now was to *force* these children into utter motionlessness, days and days and days. To his thinking, nothing proved the weakness of this class of people more than their everlasting need for action, and for each other.

His drugstore of former times had been turned into a glassed-in office in which three annoyed-looking women of the new type looked back at him impatiently. One indeed seemed made entirely out of lacquer and hairspray. Lee stepped nearer, pressing at the glass. Not for the life of him could he imagine how it felt to be one of these; he did see some little bit of fear beginning to show up in one particular face. Old as he was, he could have thrashed her to death easily with his stick. He knew it and she knew it too. Instead, he grinned, a bad grin that showed his lack of teeth. Next, no doubt about it, she would be phoning the police; Lee decided to leave.

Already he felt tired; it was one of the things he hated most about old age. He took it as a blessing that an eating place came up at the last minute, before he got mad. Three details struck him: first, there was a bell over the door, a cheery one; next, there hung a ribbon of fly-paper with fifty despairing flies standing shoulder to shoulder on it, and then thirdly, there stood an old-fashioned jukebox with, perhaps, "*Mona Lisa*" on it and that possibly, needed only a nickel to play it. Lee went straightway back to the booth that had been saved for him all these years. He had been here before, it seemed to him, ages ago, when Truman was in power. Now there was an old woman behind the counter who looked like someone he had known. He remembered a certain Naomi, famous in her day. She appeared before him now, strangling in flesh and with a face on which the decades had written with more than usual cruelty.

He pronounced his order, and then, looking at her, he gave her every chance to recognize him for who he was. Useless. She seemed dead, extinct in both eyes. Moreover, now that he could view her at close range, it wasn't Naomi at all! He found himself wondering whether he could not do a kindness to the *real* Naomi, who had perhaps gone on to the other world, by being good to the person in front of him.

"Could I have a cup of coffee, please?"

She started to write it down.

"We have waffles."

Waffles! He could feel his heart leap. Sixty years and more since he had partaken of waffles in his own hometown. And this time all the syrup he wanted and no one to gainsay it.

This was better. He enjoyed it here; he was unseen while he watched other people pouring past the window very close by. One was smiling, others talking to themselves. What consumed them were precisely those pettifogs he had finished with already—children, money, jobs—life's rubbish. As for him, he was free, also old. A boy came by with an obscene moustache on him. He ostensibly whistled, but in fact, he was thinking of women. It was this that mired the world; even Lee too, had needed half a century to clear out his own good head. He saw a woman walking slowly in greatest hauteur, letting off an odor.

He had planned to go straight back to his room; instead, he found himself taking the path west, into the bad zone where he had never been allowed to travel as a boy. There were not enough years left in him for worrying overly much about safety, and yet, seeing these faces, he was glad he had a cane and glad it was heavy. There was a fat man in an undershirt, and next, a dead cat lying exactly where Lee had seen one sixty years ago. In earlier days the sight of so much poverty had made him indignant, but no more, not now. Now, knowing what he knew, he wanted them poorer and more and more obliged to be working at all hours, otherwise one could not have counted the bestialities they would be performing in their spare time. These were those masses said to be "inert." Knowing what he knew, he would have been happy were they *more* inert than they were.

He pressed on, past a tavern full of failed people licking their wounds. It was a land of patriots—already he had espied two flags—whereas in his own view, patriotism ought be restricted to the spirit world. (He no longer acknowledged nations. What *he* saw was everywhere a sandstorm of individuals, most of them of very bad quality indeed.) Suddenly he noted a white youth looking coldly at him, as if imagining it would be an easy matter to take an old man's wallet away. Lee slowed. This could be a very good thing—he would enjoy someone risking fifty years of forthcoming life against the few months *he* had left for wagering.

The next block was full of gas stations and garages, where a soiled people were being eaten alive by cars with hoods agape. This sullen attraction between the ignorant and vehicles—what was it? Among it all he spotted a splotched woman in jewelry and blond wig with a face that showed she had never read a book. He did not like the common people, they did not like him. Anything might happen. Even with his cane he was in danger, especially if any should ever guess what he was thinking. And they *could* guess; indeed, they needed only a glance to see that nothing stood between themselves and outright slavery, save only his inability to bring it off.

Suddenly he stopped short. A child was sitting in a kind of blue-eyed ignorance in his path. Lee had seen these things before. This child, however, was lapping much too happily at the slime that issued in so much plenty from both nostrils at once. Lee reeled. He could see in this snot-nosed infant that taxpayer and sports fan of the future who was to be given as much voting power as he himself had ever had. He took one step forward, then, slowly, lifted his cane. By and large he had found that "the people" behaved better when treated from the beginning like filth. Now he was on the verge of striking this one out of existence, but at the same time incurring three witnesses. One observer, presumably the father, was striding forward quickly to protect his spawn. Lee grinned.

"What in the . . . !"

"Can you tell me where Quintard Street is?"

The man was weak. Lee's gaze had ten thousand books behind it.

"I know where Quintard *Avenue* is."

"That's it."

"You're headed right for it."

"So."

He went on slowly. In the next block was a grocery and nearby was a music shop with four or five vacuous-looking youths sniffing one another's crotches. How he loathed the young! Body-people, of all earth's creatures most distant from the truth. He could see in their faces that they thought life had just begun, whereas in fact, because they were uneducated, it was almost done. In his day these types had grown up listening to country music; now, they had taken over the tastes of the spoiled class.

He had made his tour and was back on the street that divided the poor from the prosperous parts of town. He was tired, it was hot, he wanted to get himself home before afternoon came on.

Three

THREE TIMES HE WENT DOWN, passing slowly in front of the lobby (with people watching him), and then shuffled back to his room with an armload of books. The chest itself had been parked upside down. As a result, the more immature stuff was now on top—mere novels and whatnot that he had long ago eschewed.

While his rooms were capacious, they stank of linoleum and paint. He had work to do, if he seriously planned on turning *this* into that scriptorium he had in view. First, he must people it with souls, unobtrusive types in the form of fine books. For he had as lief be finished with life at once as to go on without aid of books—if not for reading, then at least to rest his head upon.

It was on his fourth trip—he loathed having to expose himself thus to people sitting about in the lobby—that he noted one woman in particular who had fixed on him suspiciously. Lee stopped. She too had a cane, it too was heavy; moreover, she held it in a hand that was meaty and covered with freckles. At once he could feel his confidence ebbing. Nevertheless, he forced himself to turn and face her, to make his eyes goggle, and begin to pick conspicuously at his nose.

It was a bad place full of old people, invested everywhere with the smell of medicine and paint. All his days he had been a student and a reader, but there were no readers nor students here. He *was*, however, grateful for the quiet and the moroseness, the absence of that ubiquitous "music" that had done so much to embitter him. He was grateful, too, that he had been posted to the third floor, where he could speculate down on those beneath him, instead of the other way around. Perhaps most of all, he was grateful for the windows that looked, one of them, into the slum and, the other, out to countryside where even now a single plaid cow could be seen wending homeward. There was a chair, and reaching for it, he seated himself comfortably.

These last twenty years he had been reading in the Greeks, so much so indeed that he could sit in bed and summon up from out of history real happenings that most people, mercifully, could not have endured to imagine. His wisdom was increasing; his hatred, too: He now thought of himself as the unacknowledged prophet of the crumbling of the West. *This* was the good of books: for toying with Time. Old drawings in old books—he preferred this so much more than anything that was happening in the outside world. To his thinking, it were far more laudable to have been alive than to be alive, or than to be scheduled for the future. And anyway, he still thought of the Greeks as having taken to a cave somewhere, all of them coughing and nudging impatiently, all quite ready to come back on stage someday.

The first book was a little green number, celery-colored, that he cherished in his heart. This one had true knowledge in it and an author now in paradise. He took it, opening upon a little colored map so childish and naïve that it could only have been done by one of the ancients himself, someone who had actually set eyes upon the place. It was odd: He could touch down at random with his pencil point and hit each time upon a murder, or battle, or famous crime. He had also the uncanny ability of setting himself down in the empty spaces and drifting for days, as it were, from one little wretched town to the next. He simply could not understand how humans could be what *they* were while the books made by them were so often as good as *they* were. It was a puzzle. This one was *very* good; moreover, coming near, he could see where someone had made some very cogent notes in the margin and these too were good. It was seldom he had an aesthetic experience in the middle of the day, especially not with a crowd of older people, nonreaders, in the same building with him. It needed all that he had to put them out of mind, to take up the book again and then, as it were, lick, lick, lick until the ink began to run.

Frequently, he would wake to find that two or three volumes had joined him in bed. This time he rose, got out of bed, and walked around the room. The night was dark and had something in it that sounded like rain. In his time the town had teemed with crickets, now only a very few hoarse ones were clinging on. For him this was the most grueling part of the night, when he must resort to his box of photographs and, taking up one of his wife, concentrate upon it long enough and diligently enough until such time as death might or might not relinquish her up for a spell. This time it was a small square snapshot, rather faded, showing her in the full splendor of nineteen years of age. He shivered. His method was to hold a lighted match to various parts of himself, the better to bring forth the groans at once and pay the full cost here and now rather than letting it fester. Then, too, he needed to draw the attention of those who could let her out for an hour or two. One great embarrassment—the mortician who must one day see what he had done to himself.

Perhaps he could grow inured to it someday, but not yet, not now. He was weak, and trembling so much he could hardly do his work. Fainting was no good; he simply had to stop and start again. A full minute passed that seemed to go on longer than the day. He envied the dead, the sick, those awaiting execution.

There was a humming sound when she stepped out of the picture, aged nineteen. These new surroundings had her confused, however. He waited while she made a circuit of the place, blinking at it, coming back.

"Is this where we live now?"

"Right."

She nodded slowly and then went suddenly to check on the kitchen.

This now was the good time—all the rest of the world turning in to sleep and lights going out one by one. There were only a few lighted places left where someone might be working late or simply loath to be in the dark. Knowing them the way he did, he could virtually see them through walls, whole families of them sleeping in knots. One single car was still nosing from one address to another, as if trying to recollect where to berth. Also, he could see a radio tower with three lilac lights and remembered it from the old days. It was this tower that had always seemed to give the command for children to get to bed.

To his mind nothing could be more odd than that, for all these hundreds of years, so many generations had been retreating at certain specified hours into special chambers, there to lie in silence, stunned for a certain duration. As if the great Zodiac required surcease in order to plot tomorrow's day. Coming near, he saw his own features in the window, then next a much larger face in the sky, huge and wise and with an airplane toiling through its beard of stars.

He liked to rove mentally into the countryside, flying as it were at about two feet above the level of the earth. It was for this imagination-work, and nothing else, that he had been given a stint in the flesh in the first place. No doubt there was a chill; his disembodied mind, however, felt none of it. Itself, the moon, was thin (two holes in it) and looked as frail as manuscript. He could hear a train making a run for it and, further away, the noise of night animals—all of them quite prepared to perish if only they might first inflict some mortal injury. Now there came up to the window what for him was the last touch—he couldn't credit his eyes—a grinning toad riding athwart a bat.

Gingerly, he got into his gown and cap and lowered himself into bed, one withered leg after another. Judy was asleep already, as was her habit; he had always admired the blamelessness that let her, as it were, float out to sea and stay for hours in steadfast slumber. Looking at close range into that face with still so much of the child in it, so much of fifty-year-old photographs, he could not begin to envision the civilizations she had seen—pastel lands, hilltops with music, dogs more laughable than any on earth and able also to converse, etc., etc. Whatever it was, she kept it in her head.

In truth, this bed was hardly wide enough for the two of them and the books, pistol, and dictionary besides. Also the candle was weak and gave off a series of little explosions that smelled like a faintly remembered camphor from out of the past. Down below the other tenants had long ago lapsed off in the simplistic dreams of their kind, like so many low-grade films being shown simultaneously in the cells. The last thing he wanted was for his own dreams, which were complex and based upon actual historical fact, to be mixing in with someone else's dead child.

Apparently he slept, longer than usual. Judy was gone; the candle, shorter. It was yet a good three or four hours before daybreak; he could see one star putting up real resistance before blinking out forever. Someone somewhere was singing, a fine voice, but broken suddenly by the most startling sound (he could feel his heart freeze) of an ape or orangutan shrieking horribly at no great distance from his quarters.

Four

HE WOKE, FULL OF GAS. HE had two minutes to get him a cup of coffee; either that or he would fall unconscious again. As for food and breakfast, he had lost the knack of it.

He dressed hurriedly; then, taking his stick, he limped down to the "tea room" where already some half-dozen blue-haired monsters were sitting indignantly, eyes bulging, munching on crumpets. The waiter was an obsequity in a jacket, so adept at back bending he seemed to have a hinge—he would go far. Lee looked at him coldly and after ordering coffee, went out to retrieve more books. If these had been anything else in the world, he could never have trusted them to be left alone. Even so, a white dew had formed over the topmost of them. He didn't care; the condition of things no longer mattered. Indeed, so that he might leave nothing behind, he actually preferred that his belongings should deteriorate at the same pace as himself.

* * *

It intrigued him how little noise came from his footfall in fair weather. He saw a woman standing on a porch, and then, there was the same little brown dog yapping at him in high-pitched voice. These bourgeois dogs! Very brave were they in a world without dangers. This one had defecated at sighting a *real* dog from outside the gates. Lee slowed, hobbling, hoping to lure the thing a little closer. Across the way the woman was watching darkly, even as he swung suddenly and caught the dog smartly on the crupper—a good sound followed up by a cry and a yelp and a rolling in the grass. Lee grinned. The woman herself had dropped her broom, watching in openmouthed disbelief. Huge was his temptation, huge, to march across and give her one or two whacks as well, she had so many places for it.

The next block was his own, but there was still no sign of the inhabitants who might be taking up his old room, or of the woman making use of his mother's kitchen. In *his* time, there had always been a flurry, comings and goings, children playing and playing hard all day in the sun. Where were they now? His tree house had gone to ruins, nothing left to it but one or two boards dangling in the branches where once he used to scan all the way to Tennessee. He could hear television voices from several places at once. There was something ill about these latter days, something in the elongated forms and darkened homes, all of it reminiscent, it seemed to him, of the last phase of the Mayan culture, before the final visitation from afar.

He left the houses, crossed the road, and strolled the two hundred yards to the golf course. Here he had wasted must of his youth in chasing down balls for the rich, smiling for his coins even while harboring up schemes for their extinction. (If he had to specify any one greatest disappointment, it was that he had never yet witnessed that Revolution and the attendant blood-letting he thought he had been promised as a boy.) Lee stopped. Two women, rich ones too, were coming toward him with their golf instruments and wearing peculiar hats. He could feel his old excitement. Each step drew them further and further from protection and nearer and nearer to *him*. For days he had been itching to thrash someone within an inch or two of his or her life, to do it in such fashion as to alert the town that he was back, and this time with a cane.

The women themselves came by, chatting happily of interior decorating and other people's divorces. Lee followed, goggling, until one turned off into the weeds and began swiping ineptly at her ball. She didn't have to be good at this, or at anything, and wasn't. He had a view of her buttock, thirty-five-year-old material that was rather too pudgy and on the verge of breaking down. Just then, the caddie came up out of nowhere; he was a sizeable black man with a sizeable moustache. Again Lee felt the wonder of it: Strong as he was, and large, why then did he not slaughter the both of them and become rich himself? Indeed, he went off some fifty feet to give the man his chance. Neither of these women had read so much as one percent of the world's best literature and yet, somehow, had found the time to be stymied on the green. Lee could feel his contempt, an acute pain that started at the base of his skull, could feel it overflowing and filling the earth.

They went on, four of them in file. It was amazing, how the women ignored the black man, who was so much more of a presence than the two of them combined. For one golden minute, Lee thought he was about to take action. Instead, that moment, a little motorized cart came up with two more golfers in it. Never had he seen so many lips and teeth in so many Southern smiles. And so much cordial Southern shrieking! He put it down to the effects of too much prosperity too far prolonged, just as Toynbee said.

However, it was now that time in the day when his age was beginning to tell. He never came out of doors without a volume in his coat, a thin one such as would slip in and out of his pocket with a grace. This day it was Polemon of Ilium, or rather what remained of him in the form of the few fragments that had come down. He sought for and found a comfy nook with pine needles, apparently set aside just for elderly readers. Yet no sooner had he settled, than there was an insect in his underwear.

He read, slowly at first, trying to get the gist of it, especially the cruel Greek verb that had been his bane for so many years. He stumbled now upon one thirty letters long and with so many excrescences on it, fore and aft, that its meaning would be too deeply buried ever to dig out. Anyway, he couldn't read in daytime, not out of doors, not with thrips crawling in his pants.

It was hot, so hot, and yet, looking up, he wished it were much hotter still. What the world could not know was that his wife had hit upon this way of communicating with him. Lately, it had proved an aid to thinking too. He had done so much reading that he needed only to shut his eyes to see things as they were a billion years ago: the perturbed stars, a sterilized sea (thin and tenuous as naphtha), and some few gastropods (life's noblest products) tottering down a spotless shore.

He could hear a radio and, further away, a dog barking desultorily. It was but life—he knew it well—bicycles and children, business and news, a roar from deep within a shell. As for himself, he wanted to be without body in a glassine world for cultivated people, with books to be read a thousand at a time.

His own book was lying uncomfortably; he didn't care. These days he could snooze without so much as a slowdown in thought. Then too, he liked to get his sleeping out of the way before night came on. He saw now a yellow bird had come in closer and seemed to be watching, as for the kill. He had been dreaming the sun was in one place, whereas, in fact, it was in another, and never had it appeared more artificial.

He came out of the woods, staggering a few paces before he realized he was in the midst of someone's game. There was a woman, as well as what looked like a businessman in colored shoes. Clearly, they considered him a derelict. Lee goggled, leaves sticking to his suit. The temptation to do something was more than he could bear: to stop and unbutton himself, to take out his organ and piss, and to do it all in sequence, all of which he certainly did.

Five

HE WAS IN BED WHEN A NOISE broke out, a giggling it seemed, that came from the "tea room." Three hours he had waited for darkness, now suddenly he sprang up and went to the window. This opening was something magical, a wormhole as it were, that let him look at his pleasure into the year circa 1853. Sometimes he might stand for an hour, focused on a tableau with barn and plaid cow and bright blue river that scintillated now and again. He longed to hike out and plunge his hand into the stuff. The population apparently was thin, very thin; he almost never saw so much as a single individual step into view. Five million and no more—to his thinking that was quite enough, based upon what he knew, for a land mass of no matter what size. Always, he wanted a small population getting smaller, of a fine people getting finer.

Giggling again, and still from the "tea room." He felt a spasm at the base of his neck, followed by a headache that began spreading in a slow way, like a blotter in ink.

It was his hatred. Never had he achieved that toleration said to be the final result of wisdom; in fact, he wanted nothing to do with it. What he did want was an advanced torture machine with the whole world attached. Instead, he hastened back to bed and lay with his feet propped up, so that the fluid might run back into his head again.

From many indications he knew that it was time to tend to himself, lest he wished to end up with a beard, unwashed, his numerous illnesses out of control. He was starving, moreover, the product of his indifference. And there was a rash that worried him too—a pernicious infection that extended from feet to knees and that hitherto he had been trying to treat with butter and soap and even, once, with matches. As for licensed doctors, he would rather perish at once than put up with their patronizations. Also, he had hemorrhoids, so awful and long-neglected that he never allowed himself to think about them anymore.

He rose painfully then, approaching the mirror at an angle, glanced quickly to learn at once whether the nightmare of old age had lifted or not. He still thought of himself as a young man, still good-looking behind the mask that had been clapped on him when he wasn't aware. *His* old age was not like other people's; they really were old, whereas he was but going through a test.

He shaved, and then, seating himself, he proceeded to give himself a haircut. It was almost too tough for cutting. Moreover (as he noted with displeasure), his nerves seemed to be growing into the stuff, making of it an operation of some real pain. Outside, the crickets were loud now, owing to the moon, and no doubt would go on louder and louder till they collapsed; he knew them well. Night was strange in Alabama; a tree frog had taken up in the house itself, together with a giant-sized insect grasping at the screen and looking back at Lee with two blue non-coordinated eyes.

He still knew how to make himself presentable, with aid of his cane, his age, his gray-black suit. He liked to move slowly, casting severe glances that encouraged people to get out of his path. He had held on to his soul; they had not. The last thing he wanted now was to brush up against one or another of them accidentally.

Below, the "guests" had all cleared away, leaving some dozen little tables with crystal, napkins, and coverings. And food! He could have thrived for months off their leavings. The waiters, meanwhile, were in the kitchen and behaving in a loud way. Quickly, Lee went around, gathering the tips while at same time snatching up slices of abandoned pork and turkey. One person had filled a plate to overflowing and then only dabbled at it while leaving behind giant prints of lipstick on food, napkin, and goblet. There were potatoes, good ones, and asparagus in cream—he had not had any of that in years—and wine. He regretted the lack of a jar to collect it in. There was pie with strawberries, including one wedge not half-consumed and so good that he could hear himself groaning. There *was* a waitress, a blond flitch in red uniform who, seeing the threatening look he gave, remained as in a dream. He had to eat quickly, before she woke and called to her colleagues. Under these circumstances, he concentrated on the pie.

He remembered strolling out in dignity through a crowd of young people who let him through. They were weak; he had guessed from the start that none would do anything. Outside he found clear weather, a blue sea with cars instead of fish. His first notion was to veer off for the country and regions marked by the radio tower at the edge of town; instead, he found himself drawn by the city lights. In old times he had loved to go adventuring, depending upon it that the night would be full of girls. Now, based upon what he knew, the girls were, some of them, gone, and some old, and nothing worth mentioning to take their place.

He turned and walked five blocks to where a moil of shoppers was clamoring to be let inside. To him, the most unsettling part was how shopping had taken over from play; here even the smallest were milling about, hollow-eyed, one actually cuddling up to a display window for warmth.

He plowed on, working politely through a crowd that yielded only with greatest reluctance. He was the oldest there, a black element in a sea of pastel. For the first time since coming back, he began to experience, not loathing merely, but fear, the horror that he might be set upon and rent by innumerable small creatures with sharp teeth. That moment, he caught one looking back at him, a dead thing, the late twentieth-century itself in personal form, mouth hanging open.

He wanted to vomit. Instead, he came out at the side, through an emergency exit that immediately set off bells.

In his day he had been able to come downtown at late hours and find himself all alone; now the walks were full of a people that looked to him very unpredictable indeed. One had earphones, was chewing, had a bra designed to emphasize the nipple. Everywhere, it seemed to him, the female principle was in the ascendant, from literature to men fretting over clothes—one had only to compare the solemn peoples of the East with this candy of the West. Sixty years he had been away, time enough for the town to have become much, much better than it was. In fact, it was much, much worse. Suddenly he saw a horrible grinning cretin, and with him a wife who seemed constituted entirely out of makeup. He had to face it: Either these were not really valid times at all, or else his whole philosophy was in error. *They* believed they were living on the crest of history, to *him* it looked like Ottomite Egypt.

More and more these days his thoughts were turning toward collecting together the good people and setting up a new-age monastery to be given over to agriculture and books. All his life he had wanted to be in the position of abbot and to have the authority to see to it that people lived out *his* theories instead of their own. Indeed, he had already laid out in his imagination the fields, sheepfold, and the bee glade where Judy would hold sway. And a book hoard, he would have the most amazing book hoard filled with the most amazing dark books, themselves filled with the most amazing . . . Suddenly he stopped, startled by an outbreak of giggling. There were cars in the street, one of them holding a boy and a pretty girl in jewelry. He could feel his gorge rising. Even so, he was ready to go his way, and he would have done so had not the boy rolled down the window and yelled out a short statement in which Lee could discern "fart" and "old."

He stopped. He simply could not believe it, and in his own hometown, someone who might well be the grandson of one of his hiking and fishing companions of long ago. He found himself plunging desperately into his pockets for the pistol, which he had come away without. Already the car was moving off easily into the traffic, as if all were over and done with and the episode forgotten. Instead, Lee put on speed, his eye fixed upon the car with its two antennae and evil shape. His plan was to go on forever if need be, until Time and his incredible patience gave him his chance.

In truth, he had to move faster than he liked. Now, far from assisting him, the cane was becoming a positive nuisance, even at one point tippling over someone's hat. He had read of Greeks able to make good speed at age of eighty, albeit in cities that were somewhat smaller than this. Here the ambiance was bad. However, two blocks more and he found himself even with the car and crowding at the window. They had not the slightest hint as to who he was or why it was he was hovering so near—this gave him the greatest pleasure. Perhaps the boy's grandfather *had* been a friend of his; now, however, it was time for slaying. He took the cane, the girth of it. His hand had grown stronger over the years, and the black veins on it ought to have given pause to anyone tempted to offer insults.

Nothing could be more satisfying than to come home in the guise of an old man and then to track down the rubbish that had grown up in his absence. He saw another old man across the road, more shabby even than himself, but obviously thinking the same thoughts; they looked at each other. His own eyes were weak (too much reading); the other's, also, from too much drink. This precisely was the sort of material he needed for his longed-for dictatorship of the most embittered. Yet when he looked again, the man was gone!

In this section the shops were closed, most of them, and the crowd, thin. The moon was high, his own special star. He saw a bald man sitting in an eatery, trying valiantly to squeeze the last drop of pleasure out of a bowl of broth. Shortly, he would be rising and, no doubt, returning home reluctantly to a wife who loved him not. Lee knew all about him indeed, even down to his high school ring and dirty magazines. This man, too, might be the offspring of someone he had once liked. Now he was yoked to a bad wife, which is to say one who loved her children more than her man. Suddenly Lee remembered the car, the thing having gone on another three blocks and just then come to a halt at a traffic light.

He must move quickly, using his cane for an oar. One time, sixty years ago, he had come this way after a certain dance, trembling from having just kissed a certain girl; now the girl was gone, but he was trembling still. That instant, a cat came dashing up out of the alley and tried to eroticize itself on Lee's leg. These primitive creatures had not evolved in any significant way since he was a child; Lee slapped at it with his stick, missing. The car now was traveling at a somewhat more leisurely pace while inside the two silhouettes seemed to be trying to simulate a loving couple from out of the 1950's. He had to put on speed.

He was coasting alongside his old school, now a ruin and so dark and pathetic that he had no doubt but that it was full of sleeping tramps and persons like himself having come back after long careers of wandering blindly in the cities of the North. Even so, it still had a dignity to it, from all the tremendous learning that had taken place. He had memories: a society with a structure to it, teachers and listening students—all in the Golden Age of Roosevelt, Silver Age of Truman.

They were approaching the rich district (he should have guessed it from their faces). Never had he killed a rich man's son as yet. Amusingly, they still had not the least indication that he was trailing along behind, black quantity that he was, with nothing to lose and no fear of the usual punishments. Now the car slowed and turned and then began to climb among pink and blue residences with big lawns, the kind he used to caddy for. He knew them! And knew how they had turned into mere annexes of what they owned! Historically speaking, he held The Age of Reason responsible for what he saw, and the rubbishy "Renaissance." Certainly his cane was ready. Given his hardness, he almost had to feel pity for them; moreover, he had been practicing in his rooms.

They rose in tandem, Lee eighty yards behind and walking fast. Below, the golf course looked like an ocean with boats bobbing in the tide. Even at this hour a few persons could be seen, always swinging on one of the illuminated tees. People were playing tennis too; he could see a fat man in white shorts—the Greeks would have puked. He had to remember that these were America's favorite children, lest he find himself settling for mere contempt.

The car had slipped into berth; he had to hurry. The home itself was a beauty, a meet place for a Nietzsche or Toynbee; instead, no doubt, there was a wretched little businessman holed up inside. Lee found himself stumbling down a driveway lined with tall shrubs on both sides.

"Yes?"

In his day one would have doffed his hat for an old man; now, it was "Yes?"

"Lo!" said Lee. "I've come to beat the shit out of you."

At first the boy smiled weakly, and then they looked at each other. He had expected it would be the boy; instead, it was the girl who first started for the house. Lee caught her immediately on the neck, exactly as he had practiced, whereupon she gave a little leap and then a little yell. It was easy. Also there was a sweet feeling in the cane, the girth of it. Now she was on the pavement, her face reflecting the first dim glimmering of understanding in all her young life.

Always he had thought of himself as an *educator*, and like education, it seemed to him, one ought never to start unless prepared to go all the way with it. The boy seemed frozen; Lee kicked and then came down on his head. Blood. In some ways, he actually liked the kicking more. The churl was large, larger yet than Lee, but weaker too; also he gave in so easily. Lee had predicted he would. He observed the girl trying to crawl away, as if she had dreams of hiding in a bush. He let her get a few feet before stomping on her hand. (He was to remember forever the very distinctive feeling of a ring grinding under shoe.) He had not really thought to kill, but now that he was into it, and far from tired . . . Again the neck, it was this that made them shriek—neck, head, back, and buttock, and now each blow was on behalf on some great man the new age ignored.

He could have taken possession of the house, but he turned and strode back indignantly to the street. It was a clear night, blue above and blue below and numerous white stars twinkling in the well. He saw a bat feeding in a halo of insects around one certain lamp that, apparently, was more attractive than the rest. A car came by in the slow way of the rich, with an invisible driver.

He wasted five minutes waiting and watching in the woods. He might have slept, so mild was the weather. He could hear an owl and also crickets that were everywhere save in the twenty-four inch radius of where he stood. They were shrewd. Suddenly he took off, loping, cane flying, straight across the field.

Six

NOT UNTIL HE WAS IN HIS ROOM did he see he had broken his finger in the melee. Nothing so infuriated him as these problems of the body. Already one of his eyes had gone bad and was closing day by day, giving him a look of great astuteness. Then there were hemorrhoids, of course, and rashes, all clamoring for notice. One time his physical person had been an asset, a fresh new book straight off the press; now he had to run alongside to keep it from toppling over.

He devised a splint from a coat hanger wire, and then taking his courage, he stretched the thing out till it again looked like the finger that in fact it was. There was pain, trivial compared to the matches.

Old age! Nothing so wicked could have been arranged, he thought, unless it were in preparation for something very good. (He had never entirely rid himself of the hope that he might wake someday in a new place, with scope for new development). As for retribution, that was for the rich and those who had turned their backs on books; indeed, he thought of himself as in some measure assisting in these chastisements.

It was late—time to manifest Judy and give his report. Though she sometimes chided him for his hardness (wherefore he durst not tell about the beating), yet he relied on her for her opinions. His hand trembled; one full minute and he could smell the stuff begin to boil. If he could go on with *this*, there was nothing in the whole pedestrian world he could not have accomplished.

She came dressed in blue, with a scarf that he seemed to remember from the old days. He had expected a woman of forty; instead, grinning, she surprised him at twenty-five. His urge was to take her to bed, but he was unwilling to inflict himself on such a one.

He was quite happy. Going to the shelf, he took up one of the historians first; then, he changed his mind and reached for old querulous Hesiod instead. It was strange language, designed as of set purpose to keep the vulgar at bay. His eyes were so bad he had to have his wife take the book and stand off some ten feet away with it. Hesiod! He would rather dine on two lines of Hesiod than be served with the whole corpus of the Latin swill. In fact, he sometimes went to bed imagining he was Hesiod himself. Not that it had always been so easy to sleep in those days! Certainly not, not when earth was new and so much lay before it. He groaned, rolled, then sat up in bed. He was ready to fly to *any* Past, so long as it took him from *every* Present. Then, too, he was spoiled by books; the literature of the centuries had always seemed better to him than mere poor experience by the day. And in short, reality, truth, "life," etc., etc., these all bored him to tears.

He believed in a *literal* Hesiod, a Homer in the skin, and that he would as likely meet up with them where he was going as that he was going anywhere.

* * *

Somehow, waking, he found himself on the floor with the enormous table towering over him. It took some effort to get to his feet, and even then he had to make a dash for it to keep from falling over. He was not unaware of the comedy he had been putting on these last years, not greatly unlike that child who used to roll in rain puddles for the neighbors to see.

He went and prepared a pot of coffee. His scheme was to sit by the window. In fact, he had no more than settled before he saw the sun sticking up. One ray went east, flying over the ploughland and smiting the silo with a shaft of light—he could imagine all the world's cows coming to attention with hope made new. This "sun," never for a moment had he been taken in by the scientific explanation. One instant it was in a yellow mode; the next, so furry and gold that he thought of it as far advanced in decay. A bird blurted out suddenly, followed by a milk truck and a nice little man dressed all in white.

He went back and clambered into bed. He had assumed the divine Judy was in place still, until he sat up suddenly. It was a bleak room, almost no furniture, and a mirror with an old man in it who seemed suffering from "the horrors." He simply could not take this representation of himself seriously—it was not him. *He* was young, or had been, and might be so again. In any case, all these matters were but a question of will and hardness, and he considered himself the hardest of all hard men.

He had neglected the coffee; he liked to drink it in great heat, straight from the pot, a way of inciting the day to be hotter than the one before. He needed to shave—a nuisance matter. His philosophy was to perform these things quickly, and yet, once started, he found himself carrying them out to perfection. He liked to look like a patient or convict, even practicing expressions in the mirror to make it more so.

His suit itself was black. It had never been intended for summer weather in the first place, and now the sun was making it blacker. His glasses? Black too, and of a terrific thickness that had already been the ruin of one eye. His hardness increased. He was himself that one of whom Nietzsche had foretold, and with a cane that had two notches in it.

He ran down past the "tea room" and the two menials in red jackets who got quickly out of his way. Slowly and slowly, he had emptied out the book chest until now only a few contemporary novels remained, women's trash from the 1980's that he had stolen for the joy of stealing before he saw what they consisted of. He stood, smoking, watching a parade of the little people brightly scurrying past on their way to office and work. Lee looked at them and then, on impulse, fell in behind. He loved to imitate the way in which these types walked, as if they imagined something of the most inestimable value to be waiting around the corner. There was a woman on a porch, this one with humor enough in her to see what he was doing; they grinned at each other. He was moving with lubricity (he thought) until a new person (short, briefcase, sweet lotion) came up out of nowhere and left him far behind.

Really, what did they want? He had seen this throughout the whole modern period, every generation coming out with more and more handsome briefcases and a speedier and speedier folk for carrying them. He longed for that dictatorship that would blow away something of the amazing puffery of so many little people. Rather, what he really wanted was all power vested in whosoever was most embittered at any given moment. Now he could see four more coming on quickly, all of them bonded and insured, deodorized and manicured—he wanted to puke. Nor could he help but see how they went out of their way to go out of his way. He could have caned them all to death, save for so many witnesses everywhere.

He went two blocks more; then he turned in at the building where he kept his money. This was a noble pile with columns and a dome in the Sassanid style. And such somber people! As for himself, he would have preferred to be murdered by someone with a soul than to prosper by such as these. He began to feel somber too. Three tellers were there, three variations on one narrow theme, all vying with each other in not looking at him. He knew them—more interested in job than books, and more than job, in clothes. He went first to a woman; then, getting a better look at her, he switched to a man who sat looking out between his bars as into the furthest future. The second thing Lee noticed was that his fingers, immensely long as they were, were stained a vile green. Somewhere in the rear, someone was groaning softly, while out here there were icy faces only, more than he had ever seen before. Quickly he gathered up the bills—furry things with, each of them, a juiceless dignitary on it.

With so much traffic, it was an easy matter to get tangled up in the rotating door or take some injury to foot or nose. Suddenly, that instant, he recognized something, a person, someone he had known once, now in form of an old man in tinted glasses. Lee wanted to laugh; instead, he drew back immediately behind one of the columns. At one time they had done all manner of adventures together, and now Lee found himself craving to be recognized, for nostalgia's sake. He leapt out grinning, but having missed his man, he leapt back again. Perhaps it was not yet too late to go on hiking trips; perhaps it was. In any case, the man must recognize him and courteously too, else—Lee had resolved upon it—he would burn the fellow's house down.

They came out, this time face to face. Formerly, they were of the same height exactly; now Lee was taller, having read more books. Strangely, his friend too had a bad eye (Lee looked at it) and a good one that was beginning to show the first, faint, faraway signs of recognition. But Lee was disappointed: here was one person more, judging from him, who had not held on to his soul. The man blinked, then suddenly turned, hit the door, and strode off sharply down Quintard Avenue, as if he had an appointment.

They went a block at high speed. Lee could have caned him easily; he could not, however, except with the greatest effort, keep abreast with him. Above, the sun, having cleared the buildings, was spinning slowly and would soon be giving off sparks. He wanted it to be 600 degrees today, too hot for the weak, enough to melt these outrageous numbers from off the world and leave a small sum only of the very fine; to his knowledge it had never been hot enough. He was muttering about it, and people were watching. Once more, and without intending, he had been putting on a show for the vulgar, especially a grinning youth in jewelry and tattoo. Someday, surely, he would exterminate all these things in full open view, a thousand witnesses notwithstanding.

He turned in at the post office, and entered the very lobby in which he used to spend so much time studying the criminal posters. Some he recognized still, while others stirred up memories of people he had known in seventh grade. A woman was taking notes. His friend was now plunging deeply into a lockbox overly full with mail that the man himself handled with indifference.

Lee followed past five stately clerks who seemed sculpted into the wall—he could have caned the lot of them. Outside, the sun was higher, hotter, but also lopsided and still short of the ferocity yet to come. Others might suffer, for him this heat stood in lieu of conversation.

They went in at a restaurant and stood side by side waiting for a table to clear. Nor would his friend look at him anymore. Lee saw quantities of people eating, but not from real hunger; he had to remind himself of how it was in the West, where every adorable stomach must be full all moments. And it did him good to see it—that they might all be puffy as possible for the kill. Indeed, he could have caned them all and would have faced only token resistance. Suddenly, his friend lurched forward, racing quite unnecessarily for the first vacant space. Sixty years ago, they had camped together in the rain. Lee watched curiously to see what it was the man was ordering with so much forethought and concentration.

He waited, scowling and intimidating until at last he got the table he wanted; not if he lived a thousand years would he understand people who were willing to sit with their backs exposed. Now came the waitress, a giant-sized North European with sausage arms and noodles and pasta for hair. Lee demanded whiskey; then, told they had none, he decided to stay where he was. None dared ask him to leave; no one indeed had done so in twenty years, nor ever would again. Instead, he grabbed up a longish butt which someone had left behind, and smoked.

He watched three secretaries, delicate piping birds picking away with thirty painted nails. To him nothing could be more ghastly than the human face with its parts, valves opening and closing horizontally, nothing more terrible—better they had pitched the stuff in with shovels while making loud noises. He observed a table of businessmen whispering together urgently, trying not to gloat (he knew them), wasting life on matters and affairs while imagining they were doing something delicious. In fact, it was business they were doing, mere business, they knew not what else to do. For Lee, there were but two occupations for the serious mind: treason and literature. Looking at these folk, he saw that there could be no more doubt that the professions were becoming even more banal than he knew—from the great days of farming and printing and pathfinding, down now to mutual funds. The best of them looked forward to when all would be prosperous; he, to when none would be.

He felt he was walking on a seacoast in brightest weather, or, possibly, a snow-covered scene sanctified by much silence. A door was swinging but, for the life of him, making no noise. His own footfall—no noise. It was the hour when light tended to break down into its constituents, in fact, into dancing molecules that looked precisely like the diagrams in books.

According to his theory, there were billions of living people, but few who had taken on the hard work of turning life into spirit. For that, it was necessary to begin young and read widely, and be thinking at all times. As to these small people—he knew them—they preferred having surgery to entertaining a thought. He only regretted that he hadn't turned away earlier from society; now he was resigned to waiting for the next higher species to come on deck. And as regards humanity and human possibilities (taking into account the Greeks), he was never to understand why it hadn't turned out six times better than it had.

He entered the next building and searched about for the toilet, which was unmarked and supplied artificially with jasmine smell. He saw two polished shoes beneath one of the partitions and someone in them. Then he recognized that the person had taken a computer into the stall with him and was using it.

Lee came out and went down to the pretty receptionist smiling at him from the distance. So cheery was she, such cheeks, so young, he felt he was walking straight on into the arms of someone who loved him a great deal. There had been such growth in insincerity since his day, so much so that he could never be sure from moment to moment but that someone had actually taken a liking to him. There was an elevator and a button, which he hit with his stick. In his time the town had possessed but one such elevator, and it had usually been out of operation owing to so many children flooding in to try it out.

He came out into a flat area where he saw people in suits, so chilled by air conditioning that all their facial expression had been lost. Here the true purpose was to show off clothes; he saw one huffy-looking girl of the new type, with enough expensive fashion on her to pay for . . . He had seen hand-printed books that sold for less. Suddenly it hit him—that smell he had smelled before, when large numbers were brought together and all were thinking about money at the same time.

He moved down the row, no one paying attention to an old man. In truth, they *were* working very diligently, a bad sign according to Nietzsche. Horrible to be a slave, but to adore the leash about one's neck . . . ! He wanted to cane them all; instead, he slipped into the first vacant desk in order to think about it.

Here there were *two* computers, one slumbering, the other in high activity that gave off a gastric sound. Statistics too—it looked to him like the work of the Assyrian astronomers, with row upon cribbed row of sightings so painfully acquired. He was perfectly aware of the woman next to him, watching in amazement, as if she wanted to say something but couldn't quite put her finger on what it ought to be. He turned, goggled at her with his biggest eye, then reached down lewdly and shifted his testicles.

He could remember when toil of this dreary sort was considered a punishment. Now, it was the buildings that were full and the out-of-doors that was empty. Just then he spotted an extraordinarily well-dressed woman marching toward him in haste, and behind her came the same girl who a minute ago had been sitting at his side.

"Do you have some business here?"

That voice! Lee looked at her. His nose was on a level with her navel. No great difficulty at all to drive the cane in at this point and upwards, toward the throat; he could hardly credit it that she was willing to stand so near. Somewhere, a telephone was ringing. An airplane droned overhead.

He remembered getting slowly to his feet and pushing down the aisle. Some were grinning—he didn't care—while one of the older ones had a compassionate look. He had not thought he would be accompanied all the way to the elevator, or then that three of them would ride the whole distance to ground level itself. He had a woman on his right and a woman on his left; both of them, having taken up the new philosophy, looked straight ahead.

It was bright outside, also uninhabited; he had to go a full six paces to snap free of the air conditioning. These days the sun was shuddering violently, each shudder a thousand years. He knew it must be two o'clock exactly, the very minute when it was given to him to envision in his mind's eye the forests and seascapes of the lovely Silurian Age, with the sky quite cloudless where just now a few buildings had been temporarily standing. Indeed, he was like one of those proto-humans for whom the time came finally to acknowledge that they were alive and on earth without having willed it, and no way out.

Nothing could be more horrible. He moaned suddenly, very loudly. He had the most distinct memories of those days (Silurian), and he especially experienced that odd feeling of having come up over a dune to descry for the first time the astonishing ocean, vastest of things, and in a sun like this. And below? Three great cephalopoda sporting on a mint-new shore.

Seven

HE WOKE, ROLLED OUT OF the bed, and ran around the room. However, he did not feel well (nothing surprised him anymore), and soon he was back within the sheets. It was much like a hospital, this starkness of wall and ceiling. Also, the birds mocked cruelly from the window, sometimes even throwing up their arms in glee. Ofttimes he could persuade himself that he was sleeping, but not now, not today, not with the sun ripping up the roof and tossing the shingles away.

Pain in head, hair, eye and nose, nor could he remember when he had eliminated last. He had *not* become more efficient with experience; instead, he was rotting from the head down. While as to memory . . . Already he had lost the entire Byzantine Period and with another half-inch of rot would lose the Classical as well—it didn't bear thinking about.

During six days he had felt like he was pulling himself up by main force, nearer and nearer to spiritual perfection, until the seventh day, like *this* day, when he had doubts. The world outside was abounding in rumors of a Great One, a new doctrine just around the corner, and so little time for seeing it ushered in before he himself must needs depart. Or, he might envision a bright time, a tiny population of fine people, and nations governed like great universities. At present, the nations were squabbling over this and that, who should have the power, etc., etc.—he didn't care. He *was* aware of the two grand forces: wealth force and the equality force, neither of them having aught to do with the likes of him. Anyway, all the thinking he needed to do could be done in a dark cell; nor had he failed to notice how some of the very best thinking had taken place under the most hair-raising conditions. As for these moderns, they had been given the greatest freedom, true, yet had used it for doings that (most of them) it were better they had never done!

Half an hour he sat, glaring, sometimes breaking into curses. He was absolutely determined that his bodily self should serve his spiritual and not the other way around. Sloth he could endure, broken fingers too, but a headache of this kind was serious, even for the person merely writing about it. He wanted to vomit but couldn't, and meanwhile the birds, debased little things that daren't come near him when he was in his fettle, were dancing on the sill.

He was lying in a certain way, hair dragging on the ground, when the landlady (he recognized the tread) came and tapped two times at his door. He groaned. It shocked and disappointed him that anyone still had the bravery to come up here where, for all they knew, he might have parts of butchered people in his closets. Nevertheless, he rose, cursing, and padded to the door. First, he saw that she was smiling; second, that she had on a great deal of rouge, more than he had ever seen on one person, and third, that she was bearing a little covered dish with something precious in it. He regretted he had left his cane in the bed.

"Yes, we've been a little concerned, Dr. Pefley. When you didn't come down, I mean!" (She spoke in a kind of affectionate reproach, as to a child; he could feel guilt spreading over him, also his gorge rising. It did please him that she had used his title, which he had bestowed upon himself two years ago after reading his ten thousandth book.)

"Headache."

"Oh, dear! Well, I'm not surprised, the way things are these days."

"Yeah. Fucking thing's driving me insane."

"I see."

"Well, come on in, I know you've been wanting to."

"Well."

That something was bad about him, she knew, but as to *why*, that she did not know. He had money; moreover, his rooms were immaculate, stark even, in fact a desert with books. He loved to see the expression on ignorant people when faced with so much stacked wisdom. The next room was wiser still; he nudged her to the opening and pushed her in. So many books! So many untoward ideas; plainly she was affrighted.

"Now, if there's anything here you need to consult . . ." he began to say.

Instead, she shivered, and keeping her dish, she fled amid a rush of words about headaches and these times. He found himself alone, fifteen yards from bed, his rash on fire and hemorrhoids throbbing. Time was when he could snort at health and go running after the good things at full tilt; now, it was only with the greatest dizziness that he could travel the short distance to the window and, searching for his thing, urinate into space.

Eight

HE WOKE. AMAZINGLY, HE WAS *under* the bed, not *on* it; also, there was a jesting fat man in the window impersonating "the moon." He thought indeed he could see someone, the merest speck of a man trundling at high speed across one of the larger craters. Further, he could even put himself in the person's mind—a very yellow view, and a terrain as soft and strange as phosphorus and powder.

Lee came out from under the bed and then went to check in the mirror. The headache *had* aged him somewhat, a penny's worth about the mouth and eyes. Always, he had wanted a death like that of Empedocles, in full heat; now, he would take whatever he could get. In any case, he ought to die soon, before Time and Nature could do more experimentation on him. And even now, could his wife have picked him out of a crowd, an old one like himself coming up quietly and laying his hand upon her? On the contrary, he could very well imagine her drawing back in indignation. And rightly too! Nothing worried him more.

This time he was so impatient, fumbling with it, he hardly marked the pain; he was quite ready to melt the arm itself if that was needed. Now came the tears, the smell, then finally the scream (rare for him) that guaranteed success.

To his astonishing surprise she came to him this time as a child, wide-eyed, blinking, silent, frocked in green; never had he seen her at this stage, not outside of photographs, never with pigtails.

"How's your puppy? Is he all better now?"

No answer. Apparently it hadn't happened as yet.

"Want to go for a walk?"

She did. He loved to see her nodding that way, eagerly.

His first job was to stop by the garage and drain off some two gallons of gasoline. The stuff was pretty, spinning in the jar, and good-looking enough to drink. Also, he appreciated the way it balanced, and more than balanced, the two volumes of *Suidas* in the other hand.

The night was thin, watery even, and with numerous stricken pedestrians floating up out of nowhere. What *he* saw were bleached faces from out of a painting by Munch; what *they* saw was a tall one in robe followed by a trusting child. So small was her hand, it awed him how it could be that same instrument destined to be used, ten million times, for meal-preparation and patting him off to sleep on bad nights. She, of course, knew nothing of all this, and never mind that he might be bursting to tell about it.

They crossed the road and then stepped down into the golf course, a black shallow sea with ripples and threat of nibbling fish. In front was a line of trees that looked like women tearing out their hair. This was good, he liked it, an open expanse where it was quite impossible to be undone by ambush. The moon, too—formerly he used to look upon it as his own special star, now the thing was plainly in decay. Too large! Moreover, it had gone into the phase called "lilac scales." Three miles further the radio tower was sputtering furiously, telegraphing to all quarters of town that the time had come for sleeping. He did so love night and wished he had another thirty years for it, for it and for Judy, for leading her to the best authors and marrying her a second time.

They climbed the hill. She was better than he at this; moreover, with his stick, books, and pail, he was heavy-laden. Already, the townsfolk were flying homeward. He saw one little boy outracing the cars. Lee knew these habits—how in another two hours they would all be fed and televized and toddling off to bed; he yearned to cane the bunch of them. He could remember some considerable austerity when he was young; now, it was a sink of prosperity and none of them were any good.

For two blocks he followed a man who was dressed too young for his age, but then at the last minute Lee let him go his way. In fact, Lee was drawing nigher and nigher to his friend's house. Nor could he help but see how the homes were so much more extravagant these days, far, far out of proportion to what he knew about the quality of those that lived inside. He saw a woman, her face the very picture of ignorance, riding in a car six times more valuable than herself.

He crossed. The home of his friend! It was three stories high. Lee could remember when this same fellow had abided in a tiny place jammed with siblings and noise. Lee set foot on the lawn, and then he moved around to the back and up to the window itself where he saw, first, a grand-sized television and, second, four persons feeding. There was an offspring (a male, it looked), old enough to have left home years ago; he too was feeding. Lee could feel his gorge rise. It was a room without books—his friend of aforetimes who once had been a fisherman and hiker too . . . Now Lee saw something that settled the fate of his friend and offspring all: There was a landscape on the wall, one of the impossibly gorgeous kind.

He had to work fast, while the fury was on. There was a newspaper; he drenched it, using half the fluid before taking out a match. He wanted a blaze yes, a sunburn no. Nothing would have been more gratifying than to tap politely, then go inside, and explain in calm voice how and why it was the house must burn. Instead, Lee turned and broke into a gallop. The tiny Judy kept pace with him, a small and most serious person making three steps for his every one.

They went into the mountains. Normally, he would have tired, this night he was exhilarated. None had climbed these hills in years; there was not one hamburger wrapping, no condoms hanging from thorns. Although the radio tower was high, they found themselves on a level with the topmost lamp. Thankfully, the town was in a valley, the better to contain the late twentieth-century overspill. It was strange: He could see more from this vantage about the conduct of things than could those actually carrying them out. Two cars were headed for a collision, until one turned off at the last minute. No doubt there must be a full hundred of his former friends and colleagues even now bedding down under his eye. And did they talk about him ever? No. And were they fit to play with anymore? Not one.

The fire itself had passed on to other houses—never had it been in his scheme to bring down the entire city. Also, there came a dull sound when one of the cars exploded; it formed a blue-green glow that put him in mind of the matches. Probably there were humans scampering about, probably firemen at work; he couldn't see them.

They moved to the crest and then, never dawdling, they began at once to drop into the adjoining valley. Here was unexplored land, not one gleam of light anywhere to be seen. And such growth! Looking up, it seemed to him they were sighting the underside of prodigious mushrooms with fleshy gills. He stopped to take a flower, a scarlet bud much like a tiny heart on a stem. He sensed the nearness of snakes before he actually saw one—in this case, a bright green neon article of exceeding thinness flashing in the weeds. This is how it was to be roving through a dazzling painting of the Persian type, with birds of plumage and florid script running around the edges; he could feel Judy clutching at his hand. This night the moon was particularly evil and much too big, like a pomegranate cut in two, with a danger of seeds tumbling down on his head.

He anticipated a ten mile hike through darkness, then hills and the valley that would follow. It needed years to worship night in the way it deserved and to read it correctly. This he knew: He had never been serene in the light, not with all of the ignorant alert and forever busy. That moment, a jackal blurted out loudly close at hand. He had not seen fireflies in such numbers, requiring to be pushed aside. Now they came upon an abandoned shack with a curled tin roof. Looking into it, he thought he could summon up in his mind the first young couple with their few sticks of furniture, even down to the last old man whose imprint Lee believed he could identify in the bed. There were artifacts—candle, blanket, and cup. Apparently the old one had had to flee in some haste. Too many jackals, too much brightness of fireflies. The next room had a stove in it, a black personality (smelling still of bacon and pine) from the Wood-Burning Age. He could see the tiny Judy edging up to take a look.

Outside, the vines had put on a spurt—another two weeks and they would have digested shack, stove, and all. No doubt about it, the nineteenth century was ending, even if it had needed the whole of the twentieth to get it done. He could divine a path, a thin, blue, half-millimeter-wide line that looked exactly as if jotted down impulsively by a map maker without secure information. In the first place, it was far too crooked. A hundred yards more and it emptied into a "wadi" with tree roots sticking through, and some twenty geologic layers very neatly laid open to the view. He could not look upon such a display without feeling that it was time, past time, to lay him down and take up his position in the 1950's, even as when he used to pretend that he was dead beneath the quilt. It was queer how he felt so much more akin to things like this, to rocks and fossils and popular songs of long ago, far more so than to anything transpiring behind him in the city. He could see a lurid haze five miles away where modern men were devouring one another just now. And if that were not enough, the egregious Birmingham was not so far away that he couldn't see its peculiar glow as well.

There'd be but one city soon, and four hundred million in it inspecting one another's rumps. (He wanted a small world getting smaller, and a fine people living in subtlety off the ruins.) No country had been noisier than his own, nor thrown up more rubbish, and yet—he could remember the very moment of it—this was a people as might have taken up where the Greeks left off.

Here the trees were dripping Spanish moss. He passed into a clear place, and then, glancing in both directions, he darted across the highway. The tower now was flashing in great urgency; for years the nation had been foisting its methods upon a sullen world, perhaps someone was foisting back.

He realized they were running down into a channel, thence into a lake long ago plugged in sediments. He was tired. His cane trembled. The girl, however, never complained, and now she could be seen running off on little excursions of her own. He wanted to laugh. She who had set out so tidy; now, she was smirched from ears to socks. Never had there been such a person, such seriousness, so much enthusiasm of such a sort.

They found the trail and then came up cautiously to the next ridge. A truck lay on its belly, a burnt-out case deposited there aeons ago by forces he could not very well explain. Very few trees—the loam, such as it was, had all washed into the valley. Suddenly it struck him that they were being watched by a bird of some sort, which dangled just a few feet overhead. It never failed; never yet had he been able to go abroad by night without some little manner of thing monitoring on him. That instant there was a shrieking, horrifying in its essence, and so hate-filled it seemed to have something human in it. He had his cane ready, Judy came running, the moon was down.

From this elevation he could look down upon all the Alabamas, from far north (now in drought) to Baldwin County itself. It was as good a spot as any; indeed, from his stone couch giving vantage upon where the sun would have to rise, he was in the best of places for that great "Noontide" foretold by him who had been first to call for a small world of fine people. He smoked. Below were pine barrens, and then a vacant swatch where his new-world university might very well be built. He saw it as walled, with sentries, double-gated (Mycenae in mind), and joined to a clay-built hamlet with merchants and clerks enough, and new-world wizards in conical hats. One thing he foresaw clearly: after this next spate, life would be stranger than even he could imagine. One more slight falling off, then History will have turned into something never seen before.

He'd not see it, not if he stayed where he was for . . . Suddenly, he realized that he was sinking slowly into the sediment, an inch already. With him, he never could relax lest he find himself vanishing of a sudden. He might place one foot down, but then have the greatest difficulty in drawing it up. Then too, he was acutely aware of being on earth's bottom side, as if he were dangling in space.

Most were frightened by it, yet Lee was satisfied to be in a world without laws, and to have no god but the god he could make of Himself. True, his inheritance was against him—progenitors without genius or even his own iron will. Now it was late, very late, yet still he refused to turn and go back home. It gave him a pleasure similar to when he used to wait out in the rain with his mouth open, save that now it was fireflies that filled his maw and set him gleaming. He was old, old and gray, old, gray, thin and insane, and chortling in the woods. Zarathustra might discourse with insects; Lee preferred to eat them.

Let him not die at night, not when his mind was working. Just then, something reared in his path—a shrub, a bear, something in black cowl come to take his soul away. Lee spit at it and then blundered on down the rest of the distance to level ground.

Truly, it was a blessed site for the school he envisioned, good defenses from postern to moat and observatory. If he had his way, students everywhere would be living in cells, a hard regime eventuating in a small world getting brilliant. Of course, his own apartment was to be in the wall itself, with views both of the countryside without and the civilization within, and thirty little rooms for Judy's thirty ages. As for the citizenry, he envisioned them producing their own food, each taking his turn upon the wall, and so infused with all the world's literature that no modern man could endure to look one in the eye.

He'd not see it; in fact, he doubted he'd get home that night. All his life he had wanted to lord it over an unsullied place, and now he found himself actually measuring it off with his stride and marking with a stone where the refectory ought to be. He'd get no credit for it, of course—he knew how these matters went—that it would be a rich man who someday plucked his idea out of the air.

The girl was saying nothing; he saw her in one spot and then another, both times with her hands behind her back. He was quite happy. Finally, he got down in the weeds and goggled up at the moon turned beet red. An hour of this and he could make out cities, a seventeenth-century scene, a landscape painted on glass.

Nine

HE WOKE AND LOOKED ABOUT, very well pleased with himself for having grabbed off a few hours sleep. Even so, he did not try to rise all at once. The sun-wheel was high, white, and so thin he could see through it. Now he realized he had been sinking during the night, so much so in fact that he was by no means certain of escaping. Far from school or "scriptorium," he had taken up in a lime pit of some sort, with heavy machinery off to one side.

He stood, dusted himself, sought about for his hat. A crow was singing sarcastically, the first notes of a new age that was starting out perhaps a little weakly. He never felt best in morning time. He was coughing, expelling firefly wings and two little yellow lanterns. Next he pissed in his ineffectual manner, needing three episodes to get it done, with long halts between.

It *was* pretty weather, even by his severe standards. He saw clouds—one lavender in shade and of nostalgic quality, another full of lumpy books. One had spears and arrows sticking out. He could not take his eye off this lovely world, which put him in mood of a certain lovely engraving seen once upon a certain lovely old-world postage stamp. Lilac and blue, a rock formation of calcium and ambergris, a bunny with bent ear—he felt he was within an ace of reading nature's language. He saw a bush enveloped in an aura of bees, humpback creatures with bourgeois tendencies and not the slightest notion of what they were slaving for.

He had to travel a full mile before sighting the radio tower. Far off to the west was a farm that he had first spied the night before on his outward journey. Now he saw the barn was rouge-colored and bulging and looked like something out of a sentimental book. His choices were to continue on toward town, where he was certain of a cup of coffee, or of turning aside, up two hills and down three dales, and the possibility of an irritable old farmer who would give him nothing. He tossed the cane, then waited to see in which direction it pointed. Last night's adventures, he had thought, would be his last; instead, here now was yet another coming up. Truth was, he wished for a thousand years, that he might go on forever as the last representative of his generation, both those who had decamped and those that had accommodated to the times.

He came up the hill, staff dragging, leaves clinging to his vest. The farmer himself was irritable and old, even as Lee had foretold; they glared at each other. Seldom had he seen so stubborn-looking a type. Who would be the first to speak?

"Warm today."

"Little bit. But then of course I prefer it hot."

"That right? You might not like it if you had to look after a bunch of animals."

"Naw, it won't hurt 'em."

"Won't?"

"Naw."

"Kill 'em, is all."

"Not if you deal with them properly."

"I deal with them properly! Lord, man, it was a hundred here last week."

"I know that! Hell, I was out walking in it." He could feel his gorge rising. The other man had a potato-like face of the sort Lee had never liked.

"You from town?"

"That's right, yes."

"Well, how'd you happen to pick me?"

"I wasn't looking for you! Christ, I don't even know what your attributes might or might not be."

They were moving slowly toward the house, a picturesque thing if ever Lee had seen one. Also, there were horses, or rather one horse and one mule, this latter intelligent to a degree, judging from it, and sewed together out of a velvet that caused Lee to want to go over and feel.

"You've got some fine animals here."

"I suppose. That one there like to have died last week. 'Course he wasn't 'out walking in it.'"

Lee looked at him. He was bald on the knob, a palpitating location where he could have been dispatched easily with one blow of a cane.

"What is it—you sell your produce in town?"

"No sir, no, um-um, I don't go there unless I has to."

Lee nodded; they had come to the kitchen, so tidy and clean. There were pictures, a porcelain cow, a glass jar with cookies in it.

"Where do you keep your books?"

"I expect you want some coffee too, am I right?"

"Much obliged."

He had expected a good quality coffee, in fact the stuff was excellent. Suddenly he made a grab for the cookies.

"Lord, man!"

"Your wife make these?"

"Wife? Why lord, man, she died years ago."

"Mine too. Of course, she still comes back at night, sometimes."

"Good, good. Lord!"

Outside a gander strolled up, trying with weak eyes to see through the screen. It was pleasant here, with the most dappled clouds bumping in the most clear sky. There were so many notable personalities in so many forms—Judy would have swooned.

"How long you been operating out here, as it were?"

"Always."

"Always!" His mind reeled. Probably the man had meant in the intermittent sense, according to the time theory of Nietzsche.

"Yup. And my daddy before that. You want some brew?"

Not in years had Lee permitted himself any such stuff of the sort, and yet this was so neatly put up, so attractive, like a rare honey; a proper scholar could have read the future in it. He watched it flood the cup and then go swirling for a great while.

"Then I must suppose that you were out here farming all the time that I was in *there*"—he pointed to town—"attending school."

"I went to school, country people go to school."

"Oh, yes, but you don't take it seriously. I mean, for you it's simply a measure for getting ready for life, isn't it so?"

(The man nodded vaguely.)

"See? Actually, it's the other way around—life is a getting ready for books. Now where are *your* books, for example?"

"That's twice you've asked that; I'll be goddamned if it isn't."

Lee followed the farmer to the next room, which was bare and huge and, from the smell, was employed at one time for storing hay. Here was a massive portrait of a hard-looking man, with the dead eyes of the nineteenth-century set in a potato face. And below, the books. Lee started to say something insulting about their small numbers, but instead, he went over and got down in front of them. One volume of medical remedies, the rest rubbish; apparently the churl, or churl's wife, had belonged to a book club at one time. Novels (he knew them!), "relationship" novels dictated over the telephone by thirty-five-year-old, new-style authors while lying in warm bathtubs—he wanted to puke.

"Christ! You could do better than this. No, I mean it!"

"Listen, you come in here, take my cookies . . ."

"All right, all right. Show me your animals then."

He had expected a visit to the mule; instead, the man's partiality ran to pigs. Even their home looked something like his own, but smaller, smaller and more odoriferous. At once Lee waded in among them, to the farmer's surprise. It was their eyes that fascinated him, the exact same dimensions and movement as a man's, albeit backed up by terribly weak brains. One was lacking a tail, while another's ear was so perforated, so full of actual holes . . . Lee got down and touched it gingerly, as if it were old manuscript.

"Just look at that!"

"It don't bother 'em."

"The devil it don't! How would *you* like it?"

"Listen . . ."

"Holes too!"

The man was gone; Lee looked for him in amazement. Then he took the opportunity to examine the hogs more narrowly, their nature and first cause. What could one say that Plato might settle for? The foot? Because it was dainty and would have sufficed for going to a ball? Suddenly he called out in loud voice, "O ye hogs!" while rousing one or two of the males. He was aware of thirty human eyes on him, and fifteen swinish brains.

He came out, and the sun hit him brightly while he staggered about for a bit trying to get the stink out of his nose. Finally, he padded back to the kitchen for more of the drink. It was like a museum of old times here, with bottles and jars, a display of arrowheads on a board, and a fist-size fragment from another planet that was of a more perfect blue than any seen on earth. Also, a churn stood in the corner, whereon it dawned upon Lee that it was real butter he had been scenting. The butter itself—it would need an hour to find it, and meanwhile the man was striding back across the yard.

"Thought you wanted to see my stock!"

"I do, I do."

He followed, past the hogs now lying dissolved in pleasure. This time the mule went with them, or rather it went as far as the fence permitted; Lee actually found himself turning, as if to ask a question of the thing. A dog ran up then, and seeing the cane, it suddenly abased itself in the dirt. There were ducks—a whole community of them, each with a rueful little head that turned in unison with every other, all of them under command of the radio tower at edge of town.

They passed through fowls and ungulates, even to a small-size lake with scum on top. Dead waters, brown in cast, and too many huge-eyed insects sipping too insidiously at it. Next came the cornfield; Lee went into it, pushing aside the stalks, as if he knew what to look for.

"Now then! This doesn't look so very bad. Why, you should come off very well, despite the heat."

"That right?"

"Yes. Anyway, you don't need much money, living way out here."

"I see."

There was a grove and next a glade, then a well with breastwork of moss and stone. He found himself squinting down into a sanctum of blue-green ink, lovely stuff, with a drunken toad staring up in disbelief. It all came back—his own grandmother shambling off six times a day with her pail. Suddenly, he clutched at his glasses, just in time before they dropped into the well.

The farmer had edged off, gazing down at a gravestone set among yellow flowers.

"That was a good old woman, she sure was. Lord, man, *she* knew how to make this place do right."

"Look, *my* wife had four degrees. From four different universities too."

"Handle a combine! Better than me."

"Yes, yes, I'm sure she was a fine person and all that. But the kind of woman I'm talking about comes along only once every thousand years or so. Andromache and so forth. Penelope."

"Kids? Raised six of them!"

"*My* wife had only to walk down the street and people would smile, dogs come running up."

"Dogs!"

"And even now she comes when I require it. Can your wife do that? Of course not."

"My wife did a lot of coming and going, what with one sister in Talledega and the other all the way to Coffee County and back."

Useless, the man was lost in mediocre memories. And yet Lee did like him, if only for carrying on in neatness and visiting the tomb of his mediocre wife.

They were on the porch, drinking, staring into the aluminum-colored fog that kept belching up out of the lake in great plenty, like souls in gray solution. He was more and more conscious of these phenomena—fogs, abnormal bird calls, diseases of plants—as decadence reached further and further into the countryside itself. It worried him, too, how the moon, formerly his own special star, seemed to be metastasizing on the very surface of it. He drank. And crickets—never in earlier days had they sounded quite so unconvincing.

Now that nothing needed to be done (with the animals in their pens and the mule making his rounds), the farmer himself had taken on the look of an old man. He had the neatest of houses and most laudable animals, yet he was himself so bulbous and liquor-heavy, Lee could feel his gorge rising. To his thinking, the man owed it to be more like a yeoman in the ancient sense, with leather jerkin and wooden shoes; instead it was a veritable potato next to him, with belly and buttocks and little pouting mouth between two baby cheeks. Lee looked at them.

"Well, probably I ought to say good-bye now, get myself on back to town."

No answer. And no possibility of one as long as the crickets were in their snit. Lee rose, went to the porch's edge, and pissed into the begging mouth of one of the yellow flowers—he could hear the man yell out in protest.

"Ah well," (said Lee), "maybe it's just as well we're as old as we are. For my part, I wouldn't really care to witness what's coming up."

"Nothing surprises me anymore."

"Consider yourself a Kievan peasant, then try to see the Mongols riding up in great force—*that's* how it'll be."

"We never thought of ourselves as peasants exactly. Shoot, we *liked* what we were doing."

"Think of it! Greed, ignorance. All television and no literature—think! And now any one thing is good as any other. Why, I can remember when people used to fall helplessly in love."

"I remember that."

"Now these sons-of-bitches love their goddamn *jobs*, so-called, more than their goddamn wives!"

"I got a boy who's on his third wife already."

"Well certainly! If any one thing is good as any other . . . Hell, they could as easily go home with one another's spouses and never mark the difference!"

"I know it. And that music!"

"And money! Oh, how I long to grant to them the death that Crassus had—a good full meal of molten gold!" (He was losing control, the more he thought about it. Suddenly he stood and ran down into the yard.) "Money! that's it, money! They had rather *have* something than *be* something, you ever notice that? Tell me: had they rather to read in Persian or have a new car?"

"You said a *new* car?"

Lee looked at him. The fog had pushed up so far that it was with difficulty that he could see to lift the cup. Somewhere the dog was calling piteously. Never had he felt more lonely; he wished he were back in his room, asleep beneath a covering of books.

"I'm ready to go to bed now."

He had hoped for a full-size room with pictures and quilt; instead, he found himself admitted to a mere cupboard, with mere pallet. This *was* bare. There was flypaper with ten-year-old corpses on it, and in the corner a saucer of poison waited for the mice. He would never, never have been treated this way, not had his wife been still alive. On the contrary, she always saw to it that things were right. Nor could he make a complaint, not with the man already half way down the hall.

He undressed slowly, in his manner. The farmer had been gone only minutes and yet was already snoring, a wheezing sound that made Lee turn to thoughts of dough. Nothing to read. For amusement, he could only pretend that he had been transposed to one or another of the historical epochs of which he had knowledge—Frankish France, for example, when life was perilous and any little bit of warmth and security was worth everything. Luckily, the pallet did have an interesting smell. Then too, he had been left with a lamp, a sooty one that, together with camphor and linseed smells, seemed to whisk him back straightway to the Integrity Age. For him, the things of five hundred years ago were no less real than what was passing in front of his eyes. The screams were just as appalling, even if by now they were approaching the nearer stars. Time, mere Time—he could trace it back to Akkad and before, but earlier than the great inaugural explosion, he could not go. (Save that in each cycle he knew he had met Judy for the first time, the ten millionth time he had done so. And would do so again! *That* was his ace in the hole.) Suddenly he sat up. The fog was pressing, pressing and nudging at the glass.

He rolled out, went down the hall and to the porch. He had witnessed some disconcerting nights in his time, but nothing on a scale like this. The dog was calling, inviting him down the path, while as for the moon, formerly his own special star, it had so far deteriorated that it was in a different form each time he looked, like a bladder with something in it fighting to break out. He drank. The mule was alert; Lee could read it in his ears. Nevertheless, they passed one another without a word. The barn came up. Old as he was, Lee had known from the start that he would have to climb up into the loft at last to see what he could see. Nor was it lost on him what a place it was for dying, as meet as anything he could have wanted.

He lay for a while, in hay so dusty the he couldn't breathe rightly. There was a flock of hens below, and they were very nervous to have someone like him in their home. *Now* was the time to die, just now, face up under the moon and with only a tattered roof between. He could envision children gathering about touchingly, friends of his having come to sing him on his way. His soul really was coming loose; he could feel it, blunt end first. And if he expected the roof to stop him, well instead, he saw that he was looking down from above into the farmyard itself, where the dog was barking at him in great wonder. He did not feel well. Suddenly, he began fumbling for the matches, only to find he hadn't any.

He came down, past whispering hens, across moonlit yard, thence to the man himself. In sleep he looked more than ever like a potato, a grand one in a napkin, or rather, like the mummy of some lesser official on whom no great care had been taken. Four times Lee nudged before he would open his eyes.

"Can't sleep."

"What?"

"I can't sleep."

The man sat up. "Well what in almighty hell am *I* supposed to do? Think about it, man! You come in here . . ."

"Wine. I need more wine."

Lee followed him back, this time marking well where he kept the stuff. He did not like to see an elderly person in underwear, especially one of such complexion.

"Aren't you going to get dressed?"

"Hell no. Hell no, I'm not getting dressed. I'm going back to bed."

"Well, in that case, I might just as well leave."

"Leave! I wish to hell you would!"

"I won't be coming back, just thought you might want to know."

"Good! No, that's good!"

He remembered dashing to his room, gathering his things, and then hurrying back to the kitchen for cookies and wine.

"How about the lantern?"

"Take it, take it, take it, take it." Already the farmer seemed asleep, availing himself no doubt of that personal physics and lack of anxiety that Lee could not really approve of very much.

Ten minutes later, he wished he had never left. There were fens, water-logged, and a palmetto that knew how to slice. Never again would he be able to find his way to the farmer's house; indeed, as so often the case, he began to doubt there was such a person. Suddenly he trod upon something, an eel or ray in high panic struggling to get out from under foot. Mosquitoes—these he really did loathe. It required the greatest adeptness to capture even one, and meanwhile, another was always sneering in his ear. The Greeks knew them. Suddenly he lashed out wildly with the cane. Also, he couldn't stay in one place for any length, for sinking.

The moon, previously his own special star, was definitely bloated and with rotten spots in the lower quadrant. Lee groaned, his thoughts turning to his room and the books that had been wasting these eighteen hours. Old was he, tired, and hungry too, and all of this scarcely more than a mile from where he had been born.

He waded into town with his pants rolled, passing one thin wreath of smoke where a house had recently burned. He had one hour, no more, before the sun would be throwing up a new day. He, who had wanted all of life to be like certain divine measures in the music of Debussy and Ravel, saw instead that there was a gas station, an immense pile of disused tires, and warehouses with broken windows. Lee stopped. There was also a small boy with a pail, apparently siphoning fuel from one of the trucks. Lee was able to come upon him quietly and then, of a sudden, thrust the lantern in his face. The boy grinned at first, then he tried to pretend he was indignant. He ended up grinning.

"So! stealing gasoline. Can you tell me where Quintard is?"

The boy grinned. "I couldn't honestly say."

Ten

SOMEONE HAD BEEN IN HIS ROOM; she had never been able to do any bit of dusting or straightening without leaving some trace of it in an object slightly misplaced. He called twice. Too late! She had gone.

It was full-blown day now, blatant as could be. And yet, this one seemed so much like those of which he had read, with blue sky . . . he had to wonder. Someday he would go to the window to find the fields full with peasants again, and new-world pilgrims riding by.

He had not eaten, not slept; nevertheless, he went down right away to the "tea room." Indeed, the place did smell of tea, also of crumpets, deodorant, and lace. This morning he smiled at one of the blue-hair monsters, doing it so courteously she actually left off chewing. Even now it was not too late, with his suit and paste-on smile and the title in front of his name. Suddenly he broke out laughing, an unpleasant sight, and followed it up by a fit in which he spit up a butterfly wing.

He demanded coffee and a whole pie, which he wolfed down in such a way as to send the woman flying from the room. There was a retired military officer with a cane of his own; they looked at each other. The man had heft, no doubt about it, but little of speed, judging by him. Moreover, his stick was too thin. Ten seconds (it was always the same) and the man found himself unable to bear up under Lee's gaze. Never was Lee more serene, never more at peace, than when he was drilling into the soft material of some ordinary person's weak, weak mind.

He paid, stepped outside, and hit the street in bright sun. These were not people he saw, but empty sets of clothes that had elected all of a sudden to run away from home. Suddenly, he swung wildly with his stick, striking nothing. True, he might well be going insane, and yet he considered it a weakness to be concerned about such things. Now he saw that he had gone off a full three blocks in the wrong direction.

He hastened, past Alice's, and then took the shortcut behind Stewart's house. Formerly, a giant brown dog resided here, friendly to a fault; now, it was a cold-looking animal that had taken over in his place. Lee threatened, even lifting the stick and making faces—useless. The dog had nothing in him, while as for the children . . . they never came outside.

He wanted to vomit; instead, he stepped out onto the golf course and set his face toward the distant mountains. This was considered to be the most choice section of town, but what he saw were expensive homes about which it would be hard to say whether they were in use or not. Himself, he would rather see a man's brains blown out than one more tree felled. There was still the creek, thankfully. It was with difficulty that he climbed down into the ravine, and then immediately popped out again with the divine Judy. This time she was thirty in age, or forty even, and had no sooner turned loose of his hand than she began veering for the woods where were pine cones in plenty and flowers for picking.

He went on, his mind asleep. In his time, the caddies were persistently black; now, two white ones were lolling on the green. He disliked them at once—partly for their listless expressions, partly for the radio they had with them. Nothing more galled him than the sight of gum chewing, unless it were the vision of a mouth hanging open in ignorance. One boy was doing both.

"Hey!" (He put on his ferocious expression). "How come you fellows aren't in school?"

He had expected them to come to attention, but they seemed scarcely to notice. He would never understand this decade.

"What?"

"How come you aren't in school?"

They snickered.

"Whatever turns you on."

"Yeah, if you can't handle it."

Lee goggled then, suddenly, opted to change his tact.

"I used to go to school here. Years ago, of course."

"That right? Tell us about it."

"Yeah," said the other. "Like why don't you go do your thing somewhere else?"

It was a pale youth, one of the most detestable, outside of a major city, that Lee had ever yet seen. He worked quickly now. The boy's mouth was open, Lee filling it with cane. The other youth was the larger, until Lee caught him on the neck. How quietly it went! How easily they crumpled! He had one boy trying to roll out of range, the other seemingly in prayer. As to pity (so-called), he had eschewed all that long ago; he also struck the radio. Far away a man was jumping up and down, or simply playing golf . . . In truth, Lee wasn't absolutely sure any of this was happening, whether he was merely reading about it or merely writing it down.

He remembered turning, coming back for one last strike, then hobbling off indignantly to the creek. In the past, he used to tarry here for hours in search of balls; now he saw he could use it for escape. Moreover, he had utmost gratitude that the ravine was as deep as it was—no one could see which direction he chose. Judy was gone (his own fault); it happened each time she heard the sound of cane on bone.

He ran well for his age, even with shoes full of water. (He had always acknowledged that ordinary people had every right and reason to try and trap him if they could, and that if he with his brains could not stay free, he deserved whatever might follow.) Besides, the quality of his pursuers was falling off by the day.

He came out into a woods so littered with papers and plastic it seemed as if the entire town had come down one by one to cast their ballots of contempt. There was a washing machine, a tire, and close by, a condom hanging on a thorn. He went on, probing with his stick, and finally stepped out into a quiet street that he recognized. A woman was working in her garden.

She had on shorts and a straw hat; a glass of ice tea perched on the arm of her patio chair. Lee turned and then, putting on an air of frailty, began nodding in shy approval at her crop of flowers. He was old, slow—this was what they liked! He could have asked for a large-sized loan and gotten it. Across the road another old man, this one with *genuine* palsy, was watching in envy.

"Mighty fine-looking flowers you've got there, mighty fine!" He dottered.

"Why, thank you!" She loved it. She was Southern, and this was genteel stuff. He had a vision of two corpses on the green.

"Would you like to sit down? It's so warm."

"Much obliged."

She *was* soft, a mere pastry. Half his age she was, yet he could still have outrun her and outjumped her—while as for things of the mind . . . He was interrupted by a screaming ambulance in great speed; inside it were two orderlies who themselves needed the cane.

Eleven

HE GOT UP AND STRODE ABOUT the room. The window offered a framed picture of what appeared to be a Chinese scene, with coolies in the lane. Fall was coming in, no slightest doubt. He could sniff it gathering in Pennsylvania where (he envied them) the leaves were turning brown. Suddenly, it hit him he must be up and off to school again, hastening lest he be late.

Instead, he sat listening to the actual children, some of them chirping, all of them loaded down with books and apples. He saw one who might almost have been the Judy—wide-eyed, serious, taking it hard. Next was a boy with glasses that were almost as thick as Lee's own. Lee leveled at him, concentrating, trying to infuse him with a little of his own incredible strength. In fact (Lee wanted to puke), it was a plain-faced bland twit, tomorrow's businessman, who finally went up and took the girl's hand (Lee wanted to weep). And now all he could see was the backs of heads, a three-foot-tall race of the small kind bobbing off to death.

He went down and stood a moment in the "tea room" door where three monads at separate tables were squinting at one another through narrowed lids. Faces! To him they were so much more ugly than mere genitalia. He did espy a plate of yellow eggs, wonderful stuff, trembling, edged about with bacon, as well as several pints of milk.

He seated himself in dignity. It never failed with these hirelings, as if they had never witnessed anyone making use of leftover foods. He liked grits, black toast and buttermilk. Cows he avoided, so as not to become one. It was a good coffee, if not yet as hot as he wanted. Half an hour later he believed himself finished; indeed, he was actually in process of rising when the waiter tried suddenly to make off with the waffles and honey.

He trekked heavily up the stairs, not daring to open his mouth lest the honey flow. The sun had put down a big square patch with all the colors in it, now crawling in ever so sinister a fashion toward the door. His books—it pleased him to see they were getting their meed of air and light at last. For some, of course, it was too late; they had taken on the color of old cabbage and gave off a smell.

He could remember when it had been hurtful to engage in reading, destroying his eyes, whereas now he needed only to touch any certain volume for all its contents to come flooding back. Five fingers had he, one for each of the world's great epochs. Gibbon—he had only to nudge this by accident for the most amazing scenes to come tumbling out and begin climbing toward the ceiling in piles of emperors and gods. To him, nothing was exciting anymore unless it was old, written on paper, and joined to the memory-world. Life, actual life, life in the round, life—long ago he had turned his back on all that and, indeed, everything else unfolding pointlessly in a sphere of four billion producer-consumers, now shortly to be five. One time, he believed, men and women had been important—when they were thousands. In any case, with him "real time" had pretty much come to an end in the Truman age.

Next Hodgkin, eight volumes, greater by far, to his thinking, than Gibbon himself. He also had a treatise on the Euboean coinage, four volumes needing four days to be removed from a certain northern library in a certain northern county. These were big books these, while squeezed in between, in shyness, stood Henry Sweet's *Anglo-Saxon Grammar*—he had almost forgot it. Lee came closer, using not finger but eyelash, and finding that it tickled.

He liked to pile up his books and lie in them. Who read the most books, and read well, it seemed to him, to that person belonged the world. As for the little people, those who did things, carrying out activities, they were good only for doing things and should be disqualified from reproducing. He wanted a small world of sublime people, that matters should be managed as in a great school, with upper students and lower, the rest as slaves. He preferred the old tyrannies, a land without "rights"; to his thinking, no one had rights who had not written a fine book. But most of all his admiration went back to Justinian II, he who had ruled and ruled well, ten years worth and five without a nose. Or Empress Zoë—*she* never learned about life till life was old.

Twelve

HE WOKE, AND THEN HE HAD to spend the first three hours in ministering to himself. It wasn't the first time he had seen himself in the mirror in this guise, so like a Hindu in diaper.

He *was* able to manure—it came upon him suddenly from one of the stars. This, precisely, was the material he adored to be free of, asterisk-shaped chunks that had lain in him for years and with moss flourishing about the girth; it was the clearest evidence yet that he was but a man so far, and so far no god. He cried out, half in joy and half in pain. Blood was brighter in old age, also thinner; it splattered in the bowl. Had it been a public toilet, he would have left it on display; instead he flushed three times to get it out of mind and out of memory.

Next, he tended his rash, a hateful condition with kernels and milk-white heads yearning to explode. Also, his finger was growing back wrongly, so wrongly indeed that it must look very horrible to anyone who saw it beckoning in his or her direction. He had a bit of a headache moreover—he was never entirely free of them. This one was a minor affair the size of a pea. He had had very little sleep, two tenuous episodes with long stretches between. In truth, he was outgrowing his body, and these miseries were but to prepare him for leave-taking. He thought back with admiration on the young Chatterton, he who had done *his* leave-taking at age seventeen, full of bitter regrets for having delayed so long.

He had set aside this whole day for reading, now he found he was not in the spirit for it. This breeze of autumn . . . He could feel a tremendous sadness coming on. He needed time, time for cleaning up his mistakes, for having started Greek at five instead of fifty, and for having cleaved even more tightly to the divine Judy when she was yet tangible. Suddenly he started up, dashed to the bureau, and began fumbling about in a panic for the matches.

She came, but older by twenty years than she had ever been in life. Never had he seen her in this state.

"Judy?"

He moved about her in a circle, viewing from various angles. She was of the proper height certainly. Now he came close enough to sniff her hair. No further doubt, moreover she was smiling. She had come a long way apparently; there was a leaf in her hair.

"Judy, Judy, where have you been? In the anti-world all this time?"

She nodded.

"Is it far?"

"Oh yes."

"And could I come too?"

"Are you keeping up with your studies?" (The voice was deep for one so short; it always had been.)

"Yes! You bet! I'm always thinking, always."

"That's good."

"More than ever."

"Good."

"All the time."

"That's very good. And did you get any wisdom?"

He looked down.

"Never mind, that's alright. No, really."

"I've been killing people."

"And you'll have thousands and thousands of years, for wisdom and everything else too."

"You say so. But is it really true, Judy?"

"Oh yes! And more than that!"

"And books made of glass—is *that* true? To be read six and seven at a time?"

She laughed in great merriment and then, a gesture from the old days, tested his forehead with her palm. Only now did he fully realize it, that she was in Mycenaean dress. He saw her glance at the clock.

"No! Don't you want to lie with me for a while?"

"We'll have thousands and thousands . . ."

"But will we be able to lie out in the field, like we used to do?"

She laughed. "Well . . . *approximately* like that."

"'Approximately.' Alright what's it *like* over there, I need to know *now*! *Now*!"

"You'll like it, I promise; especially will *you* like it."

"Because of the books?"

She laughed. "Yes. And much else besides."

"But why can't I come *now*? *Now*!"

"Oh! you know very well. Because there's still so much to be learned."

"I already know it all!"

"Not altogether, no. For example, there's a man in Munford—forgive me, Lee—who knows more than you!" (Again, she looked to the clock.)

"Wait! I've been wanting to ask . . ."

"Yes?"

He had forgotten what he wanted to ask. "What Munford man is that?" (He could feel his gorge rise at the thought of it.)

She laughed merrily. How handsome she was in chlamys and tiara! Outside a car was moving past, radio at full blast. She had still the most pleasant shape—he wanted to *hold* her.

"Wait! Can't we lie down for just a little? Till you count to ten?"

She smiled, already fading somewhat about the edges.

"Judy! Tell me, will we be young?"

"More than young." She came up, squeezed him, then . . . was gone! Instead of Judy, he found himself pressing at the blank wall.

Thirteen

IT WAS SMELL OF BOOKS THAT PULLED him to the library, a two-mile distance through buildings and in and out of the post office where he dallied over certain posters. The streets were virtually empty; two months ago it had been heat: now, apparently, they feared the possibility of cold. Someday would come the last summer and last cold, as ingenious new diseases swept the land.

He turned in at the building. He then approached the desk and the librarian herself, whom he abhorred upon first sight of her. Never read a book, this one—one need only look at her. And belligerent! He saw all: Not only was she keeping the books in tight sequestration, but she was mutilating them in her spare time.

"Pardon, might I apply for a library card?"

Her mouth tightened. Clearly, she wanted to reject him on the spot, but unable to find grounds for it, she took out a form and slapped it down. He had to take off his glasses and bend down close for the tinier print.

Information they wanted, far, far more of it than *he* was likely to give. Finally, he turned it back, expecting to be graded; instead, she slipped it in a drawer.

The building was deep and ran down into an angle where he had never dared to go as a boy. He went there now. He saw a woman who was knitting, her legs too short to hit the floor, while another was splashing happily through a scandal magazine. This is what they loved—the immoral activities of the rich! He didn't know whether to snort or allow his gorge to rise. The collection itself was not hopelessly bad, not until he got to the fiction and actually opened one of the things. Truly, this was amazing: 500 pages of fill. Now he saw the trouble—a portrait of the author herself on the cover. Some of these people actually seemed to imagine they could stand in the same circle with Wolfe and the others, as if the period of integrity had not all long ago passed over into mere publicity and busyness. He wanted to puke. Here, in a country like this, the commercial motive had long since eaten all the rest.

He passed on, into the disused region where history was stored. This was garbage too, most of it—mere academic-career writing, and shelf after shelf of America's poor paltry two minutes of record and middling personages. Jefferson! *This* is what the world needed, a new biography of Jefferson. He could fly by all this in perfect safety, to Europe next, where he slowed, and then halted. He knew for a fact the fourteenth century had a hundred years in it, whereas here were only two thin books. Small wonder they could not recall this century if they could have so easily forgotten the 1950's. It was not till the fifth century that he really began waking up. His good eye fell on Salvian first, a timorous-looking little volume that hadn't seen the light since . . . Suddenly he descried two stripes on it where the woman had been carrying out her punishments.

He possessed one version already; nevertheless, he made the decision now to salvage this one as well. It was his luck that one of the women glanced up to catch him at it. He scowled, at the same time dropping back under the staircase among Greece and Rome. At once he spotted old portly Herodotus, a good man; Lee found himself smiling back in return. Indeed, they knew each other well, Herodotus and Lee; one because he had seen Egypt when the pyramids were young, the other because in dreams he had seen them turned to dust. He smoked, teetered, drew back yet more deeply under the staircase. Really, he ought not come to libraries, Lee, not with a fever like his for all that was old, gone, past, legendary, written on paper. He wanted an old world getting older, a scarce population getting scarcer. His mind flew back to predemocratic times, when the wise of the world knew to treat the masses for what the masses were. Suddenly, he plucked down volume one of Herodotus and opened by divine chance precisely upon the False Smerdis section wherein the Nearer East found itself in great uproar. (He called the chance "divine" inasmuch as only yesterday he had seen a man downtown who struck him as having the very features and very limp of Smerdis himself.) *Now* it all came flooding back—Smerdis, the insane Cambyses, etc., etc. This was *real* stuff, real, and quite altogether in a higher category than the nonromantic, or rather, antiromantic tendencies that had followed so hard upon the heels of the—to Lee's thinking—rubbishy "Renaissance" and even more rubbishy, which is to say even more rational, "Age of Reason," properly so-called. Himself, he loved romance, romance only. He knew this about his century: no romance. And never will there be any, where majorities hold sway. Therefore, Lee stood ready at all times to throw the last five centuries quite away.

The next range was to have been on the Assyrians and whatnot; in fact, there was nothing whatsoever. Three times he went to the wall, feeling, taking off his glasses. Not only were there no books, no shelves to put them on! Lee cursed; he had to cross an aisle, a domain of cookbooks on one side and dieting on the other. The librarian was facing him, while at the same time, barking over the telephone. He approached cautiously and then, with all his courtesy, which was considerable, lay a diet book under her nose.

"I'd like to borrow this, please."

She snorted. "I'm sure you would."

"I would, yes."

She went back to work.

"May I?"

"Certainly not."

"How can that be?" (Clearly, she was enjoying it.)

"First, your application has to clear. Second, you . . ."

"'Clear?'"

She sighed. "First, your application has to clear. Second, you receive a card. Third, it has to be laminated."

"'Clear?'"

"We have to contact your references."

"I don't have any."

"Ho!" She went back to work.

"Do I get the card?"

"Absolutely not."

He looked at her, her eyes sparkling in joy. Now he remembered the stripes and the extreme meekness of all those others in the building.

"I'm thinking of beating the shit out of you."

Normally, he would never have been able to leap the counter, high and broad as it was. At first, she seemed to imagine he was trying to dance with her; she was even wearing a sickly little smile. She *was* large; it summoned everything he had to put her on the ground and then, while she lay in wonder, set the cane under her chin. This was by far his most favorite position, to apply all the pressure he wanted by using one knee alone—he wished only that he had the whole world at the same disadvantage, all through the magic of *leverage.*

"Succubus! Alright, just tell me this—and this is as easy as it gets for you—who was Galla Placidia?"

Nothing, she had no slightest notion about this nor anything else; he could see as much in her mammal's eyes. Lee increased the pressure. Three of the ladies had come up politely and were peering into the pit.

"Goddamn it, you've been abiding here all this time with all these books, and you've learned nothing. Nothing! What *have* you been doing?"

"Working, she's been working," spoke one of the ladies.

"I see. Working when you could have been reading." He increased the pressure. "Well then, tell me this: who was Prosper of Acquitaine?"

"*I* know."

It was the knitting lady. Lee didn't call upon her however. The librarian was now beginning to suffer in truth, obvious from the way her feet kept thrashing. Curious how completely she had surrendered, and what a fine person she might have proved, had she but met up with him sooner. Suddenly he took away the cane.

"Now hear me well: I'm returning someday, maybe a year, maybe tomorrow, and you had best *know* something. You mark me?"

She nodded. He even felt a sort of pride in this, his first real student.

"Remember!"

"I will."

"Swear."

She held up her hand, a pudgy one with rings. It now took the greatest effort to get back over the counter; nor did he forget to rip out the telephone. Amazingly, two of the ladies had gone back to their magazines. He took the Salvian, showed it to her, then went to the glass door and the world outside. It was fine weather, and yet he had not gone a quarter of a block before something cut across his view in the form of a tall benumbed boy with earphones, mouth hanging open, T-shirt with inane slogan on it. Others were straggling along behind. Lee could see a mile in either direction, and yet—it came to him in a sudden feeling of sadness without end—he was himself the only one in sight to remember what it was to have lived in a real country once.

Fourteen

HE RETURNED TO THE HOUSE, wending his way slowly after so much work. He had visions of a nap, a moist one in which he might lie in perfect unconsciousness for three or four hours, and then wake with a great clarity in his head. But first he would visit the "tea room," with its cleanliness and numberless good things. Suddenly he broke into a run.

It was a police car that made him stop, a most untoward manifestation with an insignia on the door. He hated to see these things at his residence; indeed, for one brief moment he had the horror it might be that same humorless young man who had arrested him in '49 and '47. Immediately, he turned and went the other way while behind him, in the vacant car, a radio was giving off the sputtering commands of some nitwit downtown who couldn't so much as frame a proper sentence. This time Lee wanted no woman on a porch pointing and giving him away, as in '47. Faster he went, then, seeing he had excited a little dog, slower. Even after his nose was safely around the corner, it was still not too late for a bullet to come crashing into his rump.

He made a circuit of the block, moving in high dignity, then he turned into the alley. What staggered him was the sight of a fat man of huge ignorance framed squarely in his window, his loutish hand wrapped around a book. Lee had to change glasses to determine whether it be Hesiod or not (it was) and what the man was doing to him. Another such person was roving in the interior, no doubt handling his other possessions as well. Lee shivered; twenty years ago he might have taken on the both of them, but not now, not against 400 pounds, not even with a cane.

He did debate about the car, stealing it, but he had by now probably lost the art of driving. Upstairs, the man had taken up another of the books (Schopenhauer it looked) and was turning through it painfully, page by page, hungering for wisdom or, mayhap, clues. Lee calculated he had either to escape now and promptly, or risk, not so much the mild proceedings of '49 and '47, but of being handed over to a crowd of aroused Southerners. He knew what *they* could do.

He came out of the alley at high speed, around the corner, and past the house. Upstairs, the man had still another hundred pages of Schopenhauer, all of it in pure German, and other volumes besides. Again came the dog, once more threatening to break into noise should he step too fast. Lee was acutely conscious of his abandoned room and books—all of it now seized by two men whom he had no power to chastise. Indeed, it seemed unfair to expect it of himself at this age, when he was fit only for women and children, and then only with a weapon.

He aimed straight for downtown, even cutting through the cemetery to arrive the sooner. Here was a fresh-made grave; inside it were two living men joking over their shovels. Rare was it, rare that Lee caught anyone at such a disadvantage. And such an opportunity for urinating! Instead they merely looked at one another. Next was a vault, a sculpted business big as a house, all of it intended to prove, no doubt, that its tenant (now down to bones) had had much money one time. Vanities aside, these were the only people who knew something he did not. Perhaps if he got down and pressed his ear, here where a seventeen-year-old was lying radiantly in rouge and robes—perhaps *she* knew something he did not. Could aught be more strange? She had been but a naughty little girl at the time he was himself already being arrested. Lee scanned his memory, finally coming up with one brief glance at a certain wan face watching out of a window as he was driven off to jail.

He burst out the gate, then down in front of the library for the second time that day. Remarkably—and this gratified him more than anything in years—the librarian was reading, and reading well, to judge by it. He found himself swaggering, past the post office, then the bank itself, with its reverential interior and specters that moved back and forth. A policeman was assigned here, one that seemed rather more intelligent than the mass of them. He had an unblinking gaze that, according to the uncanny intuition of these people, settled precisely on Lee. Lee hummed, grinned, then, suddenly, whipped out his account book, which had a quieting effect. The clerk was middle-aged, with sweater and nipples and a smile that must have been warm at one period but now had something sour in it. Never in this world had she thought to be still here after so many years. Lee grinned. He did not approve of her hands, or that they had grown so much larger than the rest of her, like garden gloves with nails pasted on. More than that, it depressed him that they were so willing to let his money go when they ought to have tried to have it stay.

He took all of it and then retreated behind the column. He had wanted mint-new bills, whereas, in fact, some of these had been passed around, person to person, as far back as '47. He did have some of larger denomination, the bulk of his holdings, a year's worth perhaps.

He went five blocks, in and out of a pale people with ashen faces. Up to now it had been summer and fall, sweet times all, now to be followed by the horrors of an Alabama winter. Leaves were scuttling; some were brown. Also there was a good man hastening home whilst holding to his hat. Blustery weather it was, out of the north; holding to his coat, Lee let it waft him to the corner and spin him around. Now he was facing the slum itself, a wedge of brown manure that blocked off the horizon and emitted smells. Somehow he had known from the beginning he must end up here, even from the first time he had strayed out of his own good precincts and wasted an afternoon touring the place in 1948. *Then* was a dead cat in the gutter; *now* a drunk man sat in his route. Lee stepped over him.

Previously it had been a thoroughfare for children on their way to school, whereas now, the population thinning, the children having grown up and gone to Birmingham, it appeared to be going back to weeds. He could recall when the poor were in full flower, numbers of them dressed out in the nobility that comes from wanting only a living and having a hard time getting it—all gone to Birmingham. It was old people he saw now, leftovers from the '40's and '50's who seemed genuinely ashamed for being still alive. He approached a theater where a line of unspeaking and sullen old men stood waiting to see James Dean.

It shocked him too that the slum was as diminished

as it was, a mere residuum of twenty acres worth and with apartment houses of the new type nibbling at the edges. He had to remind himself it was daylight still and not the early evening suggested by appearances. Here, in winter, nights would be long indeed, the sun small and far away. For the life of him he could not imagine why he had checked into the "tea room" in the first place, not with an authentic slum next door. He wished to die in a place that was meet for it, among a glum folk that needed none of his punishments.

He saw a boy with cigarette burns for eyes, while on the porch his pregnant sister sat singing hymns. He preferred his poor people to keep silence; in fact, he preferred *everyone* to be poor, saving only a few seers in great estate. It brought back to mind the time when he used to be able to peer into the homes of the poor and spot every time a sick person lying on a couch. Then he noticed a young woman with *two* babies, both in worse condition than he was himself. For it had come to this: that he loved those only who were striving always, and always failing.

He rounded the corner, and then, seeing where the poverty stopped and the blandness commenced, he turned and came back. He could step across this tiny demesne in minutes, from the corner store with the wood-burning stove, all the way down to the nasty little park full of drunks. Someone had been tossing out sanitary napkins; never had he seen quite so much evidence of so many bleeding women. A dog was carrying one of them as proudly as a bone.

He had a choice of two hotels, one, a red structure with failing spine. It was not so very high, not when compared to what he had seen in big cities, yet high enough, he thought, to let him look past the ramparts of the town. At once he went in and lay his cane on the counter.

"I'd like to see one of your rooms."

"Would?"

"Yes. If I might."

"You might *not* like to see it—once you've seen it."

A wag, the first he had come across in his whole journey down south. Moreover, as if that were not enough, he had a chess set on his desk.

"Do you have a room at the top? Whence I could see over the wall?"

"Top floor's full of niggers."

"I don't mind."

"*They* mind. However, they only come out at night."

"Well, how about next-to-the-top?" (He had started to say "penultimate.")

"Oh yes, I think there's a floor there."

Oddly, Lee found himself grinning as well. "And does it see over the wall?"

"Let me understand: What now exactly is it you want to see over there?"

"Well! That I might view the sun once in a while."

"So's he can 'view the sun once in a while.' Gad! Alright, as you wish, come on, come along."

Lee followed to the elevator, an unstable contrivance with a spittoon in the corner. They were traveling slowly in the extreme, and the pilot wore a grim expression. Lee was hardened to graffiti, so he believed; still, it amazed him how someone had inscribed on the very face of the escarpment now passing in review. He had a sight of the third floor, the rooms closed off, not with doors, but blankets and hanging shawls. He simply could not credit it, that such an institution had been doing business all these years in the same town in which he had grown up.

"Have you lived in this town your whole life?"

"Don't know. It ain't over yet."

Useless, Lee could feel his patience waning. However, the cage was too tight for using the cane. The next hall was darker and more narrow still, but equipped with doors, as Lee was glad to see. Footsteps overhead. He had the impression that all noises had fallen silent the instant he stepped out of the box. Now the wag was gesticulating for him to make it quieter still.

"Sssssh, Gorblimey! Look, some of this trash is on night shift."

"Night!"

"Sssssh!"

They went to the right then. The wag took out a key and tried it, turned and came back. The first good circumstance was that the place did have electricity, also a light that worked. There was a bed, rather sad-looking, and not much else. The room *was* long, the way he liked, and did have a niche to it; he reckoned the free space as enough and more than enough for all the books he was still likely to collect. Best of all, he saw a window, or porthole really, that looked down through smoke and haze directly into the very district in which he had grown up without once suspecting that he could be observed. He had a great impatience now to be left alone.

"Yes, yes, this is fine, fine; how much do I owe you, as it were?"

The man pondered, doing numbers in his head, then finally coming out with a sum that Lee paid at once while inadvertently exposing his money. Even now the sun-wheel was dropping behind the barrier and would soon be gone.

"What about your belongings?"

"Have none."

"You don't have any *belongings*? The kind of money *you've* got?"

"I'll get 'em tomorrow."

"The rood! 'Tomorrow,' he says."

It seemed he would never leave. Finally, Lee raced to the window. He had hoped to view children playing, even, if possible, a dark-head urchin in a scene from the '40's; instead, he found himself scanning the edge of town with fence and tower and, beyond that, where his eyes gave out, cornfields green as paint. The sun itself was globular just now, or rather, the more he looked at it, a knot of snakes. He liked to take it on the tongue, stingingly.

In fact, there was just light enough to let him see the room in its true horror, a thing of wet brown plaster with a bed so narrow it looked like a trap with teeth beneath the sheets. Someone had died here recently; his old man's instinct told him so. He was loath to sit, loath likewise to move down into the darker part, which seemed to extend on for a considerable way. No books. Finally, he did sit, but on the floor, one full minute before leaping up suddenly and snatching away the veil from off the bed. It was *not* a griddle, not wired, not a stove, merely a mattress with spurs sticking out. He pressed once with his foot, sending up a spray of dust and pollen and the stink of activities for which no agreed-upon names had been devised.

He remembered dragging it out by force, down the hall and to the stairs. Here was a window that looked directly into the core of the slum where already congeries of neon advertisements were spitting and hissing and giving off the sort of granulated light that he recalled from his own dear epoch. So many years! He *ran* down, cane clattering, then drawing up in dignity before marching out past the clerk.

If it were dim upstairs, here below it was actual night. He bumped into a beggar, who bounced off and then stood grinning at him through blue glasses in which Lee could see a magnified reflection of the moon and its pits. Behind, the first of the black people were coming out quietly, one by one, looking in both directions. It was an evil night, with fog, or a gas that kept changing in shape. Moreover, the gate had been closed and bolted, and a tall man had taken up guard with what looked like a blunderbuss and tin hat. Somewhere he could hear a radio—so he imagined—playing the old programs.

He crossed the street, went a block, then stepped into an eatery that remained very dim in spite of the neon. Here were booths, people smoking, a whore at the bar—precisely the sort of sight and adventure that sixty years ago would set his heart pounding. Those days he was too young for such places; now, too old. Now he asked for no greater windfall than an empty booth and found it, but then made such a dash for it as to bring down more attention upon himself than he wanted. True, the situation was excellent, the best in town; he could see everyone, and no one could see him. He rather liked the smell of beer, while here and there he caught sight of a face of so much thoroughgoing ignorance as to take his breath away. One was looking at him haplessly, as if asking not to be judged with too much harshness. Lee looked at him coldly at first, but then began to soften. Here was perhaps the last place left for him where he could still feel pity, here among the *truly* poor and the *genuinely* ignorant. Next, the man was gazing down at the floor, revealing that he had big ignorant ears as well. Suddenly, Lee began digging for the matches, so as not to have to describe it for his wife later on. As for the whore, this one was already too old for it, it seemed to him, yet seemed also just starting out.

He had rolled his sleeve and was doing his work when the waitress came and caught him at it. He grinned.

"Oh, Lord!"

"No, no; this is the least of it. Could I have a menu?"

It was his age that saved him, age and his suit. At once he began ordering, faster than she could write it down. Outside, two black men had come up and were peering in uncertainly, still not quite yet entirely willing to step inside. He could see the tower, miles away, where one of the lights had gone out. It had been weeks since he had had an aesthetic experience; now, between the smell of food and beer, bad music and ignorant conversation . . . Sometimes he could sit smiling, his work-ruined hands clasped benignly over the massive head of his oaken staff, could do all this even while the reality around him dissolved into pure Idea. He was so warm, so deep in the building, and the building was so deep in the slum—no one he had ever known would dream to look for him here.

Fifteen

HE WOKE, GROANED, BUT THEN got up very quickly when he saw he was on the floor. It was a brown day, the beauty of it pulling him perforce to the window. He saw a speckled scene of great mellowness, with leaves, corn, and tiny red sun. At one time, people used to hold themselves in readiness for just such days; now, it could be seen on television. He opened the pane and stuck his head out, but then had to draw back in quickly when he found two other old men doing the same. This breeze! He could identify apples rotting and the smell of burning pine from off the hill; all his life he had carried his wisdom in silence that he might at last measure up to the beauty of things. Down below were five billion people, each representing one brief opportunity to turn into soul and survive forever. They were failing; he was not.

He dressed slowly, humming, finally trotting down to the unspeakable little bathroom with its defunct toilet. Here were writings, one of them detailing a certain craving that even he in all his travels, not even in Mexico, had heard described before. He checked the mirror, still half-expecting the thirty-, or forty-, or perhaps the fifty-year-old that he used to be. He needed a shave, needed coffee, needed a new suit and brighter shoes. Suddenly, he was aware that he had left his cane behind, a hideous realization that sent him reeling back to his room.

He went down in an optimistic mood, although shunning the elevator. His wag of the day before had vanished, and in his place a henlike woman sat indignantly. They looked at each other in open distaste, both on the verge of saying something about it.

Outside, it was clear but plain and not nearly so autumnal as from his window. He never knew whether it was the climate or his own spiritual condition that was in play. He passed a humpback creature who would have stirred pity in him yesterday; now he was more conscious of the money in his vest.

He traveled three blocks before he remembered there were no bookshops in Alabama. He did see a furniture store full of second-hand items that, most of them, he would not have thought to be saleable, all of it under the direction of an aggressive little woman with makeup and perfect breasts. He judged her exciting, for anyone with libido.

"Very good! Tell me, do you deal in *mattresses*?"

"We have, yes, you want mattresses?"

The accent, Lee judged it of Portuguese and/or Spanish origin. "I do," he said. Then: "Well not mattresses but mattress. I have one, you understand, but need another."

"You want two mattresses."

"No. Actually I . . ." She was fast; he had to follow her back through three rooms in a row. At the end, he caught sight of a hobo from off the streets rummaging about through racks of used clothing. Here the mattresses looked in worse condition than the one he had jettisoned. Some were crushed, some bent, one soaked in blood.

"Would you have any that are *new*?"

At once he saw his mistake. The woman came to him.

"Do you see anything here that's new?"

"No."

"Rugs—are *they* new?"

"No, they're not new either." In fact, he felt proud of his right answer. She was so much like a teacher he had once had, hands on hips; even with his cane he felt quite powerless.

"Those—are *those* mattresses?"

"No, those are tables. Look, you'll be old too someday."

"What? What you say? Okay, buster-man, that's it, that's all for you."

He found himself being escorted past furniture and dresses, past the hobo who seemed to be snipping off the buttons and putting them in his pocket, past all this and to the street itself. He could have taken her by storm in his youth, now she was on the sidewalk shooing him away.

"May I remind you . . ."

"Go! Go!"

The day was pale now, with fumes over the sun. He went on slowly, speaking to himself, then suddenly, of an inspiration, he turned into a small place where the smell of coffee was brewing. He always wanted a separate table for himself; here, the room was full of tramps shoulder to shoulder in silence, as if ashamed to be seen in each other's company. Lee squeezed in, not without difficulty, between a black man and a white, both of them pretending that they were not being more or less roughly jostled by a third man with a cane. Soon enough would come someone to give out food—he was confident of it—and meantime, he was happy with the silence and proximity of two or three others who seemed to be of about his own age. They blushed, stealing looks at one another. These were not highly developed persons; not one of them could have passed any of his tests, and yet he felt the presence of at least one other soul in the room, even if he could not have pointed to whom it belonged. One man looked like Dostoevski; the soul, however, belonged to someone else. Another was so brutalized, so lacking in one ear, he would have made Prime Minister in the punishment state Lee envisioned. Just then Lee spotted a wily fellow at the back. They were, all of them, of that tiny minority in Time called sometimes "people," and sometimes "the living." He knew for a certainty they would turn and rend him if they but knew what he was thinking. Indeed, he was on the point of leaving when the woman (tall, austere, expressionless) made her appearance and began to go around with her cart. He had expected a sorry food, a weak soup at the best; in fact, it was authentic meat they were given and with a choice between turnip and potato. Lee took it gratefully and threw it in. There was bread, and it so good that he was ready to give worship to any god she could point to. The men were in a frenzy, as he saw, all of it out of the ten-billion-year-old dread that someone might come and take away their portions. Nor did it matter that he had read hills of books and had a "Dr." in front of his name.

He remembered the bunch of them rising silently one by one and filing out without a word. One man had left his tobacco plug—Lee didn't want it. The last he could recall it had been summer, now there was a cold chill that went straight to the bone. He saw a woman so bundled in coverings she looked like blankets in motion. He had observed it before, how that, for the uneducated, life was finished as soon as youth was done. There were no police here. Instead, he saw three black men standing back to back while watching the street. The woman in blankets, she was not Judy in spite of her correct height. Nevertheless, Lee turned and flew off around the block to catch her on the return trip.

He no longer expected anything from this weather, not with winter coming in. The sun itself was but a fluff of seeds held together with spider string. It was strange: *he* was on earth looking up, and yet at same time he could easily imagine himself on the sun looking down. He saw a spindly man making toward him, a mere lacework of atoms and open spaces and the averted expression of one who finds himself suddenly on the wrong planet. Lee dallied, smoking, while figments of literature passed through his head. Behind, one of the shopkeepers had come out and was trying to intimidate him into going away. Lee grinned, drooling on purpose. He felt this way: he had nought but his cane and seventy-two years, yet he stood ready to contest with anyone that wanted; he knew it they knew it. Therefore the wisest of them made a grand detour to keep out of his way.

The woman, when she came, was not Judy at all, who had kept pretty to the end. This was a hardened person, and there was no way on earth to get a close look at her without causing an affront. She stopped, stamped her foot, then began cursing in a bitterness out of all proportion.

"Pardon."

"Pardon, shit! I ain't your goddamn long-lost love, Jesus!"

It was true; he backed off apologetically. Suddenly, he grabbed for his money, finding it all intact. A bus came up, and the driver looked at him with so much impatience that he felt obliged to step on board. Three things he noticed at once—that it was warm, that it was loaded with working people, that it smelled of fuel and dirty clothes. All his life he had gravitated to the rear of buses, always hoping to find the last bench free; instead, this day, a melancholy black man had taken the best of places and was gazing out in such a way as to show that for him it was too late and nothing would bring back his enthusiasm ever. Lee nodded and then, getting nothing in return, took the window opposite. It gave a good view of the road, yet within a minute he felt himself lapsing into a kind of slumber that was a great deal like reading, with stores and shops passing by. Here was poverty in truth, enough of it to supply the most optimum field for spiritual development, as Toynbee said. His own most favorite ages, certainly, had done well enough without prosperity. But not without slaves! Indeed, he saw everywhere thralls in thousands, a lost people whom history had cheated of harness and lash. Even now one of them was gazing back at him, a largish man, a voter and sports fan, with massive skull.

Lee preferred them in poverty; he had *seen* the conjunction of ignorance and wealth, as well as all that nightmare of the 1980's. To his thinking, the slum was only too small, too hemmed-in by its egg-shaped circuit roofed over in cellophane. The young, those that were shrewd, had all long ago scrambled over the wall on the shoulders of the less-shrewd now standing around casting shadows. It had always been difficult to prove to the prosperous that they were in fact ignorant, whereas here . . . These non-prosperous ones seemed almost ready to listen.

It was then he saw something that made his whole philosophy teeter in the balance—a tall man standing to one side while keeping his face from being seen. Lee had always understood that if ever anything should actually happen, it would be owing to some quiet person who kept his face hidden, had a pitiless will, and a head full of lovely brains. He could hardly restrain himself until the bus stopped and he was able to cross and come upon the man from behind.

It *was* an interesting face, bony, with speculation in it. Lee had been accustomed to believing that only Eastern people had somber faces. As to whether this was the One, the *true* chastiser, the *Flagellum Dei* for whom Lee was but serving as herald—he wasn't so sure. Now he must either grasp the man at his belt or let him get away forever. (For a long time now, he had been aware of rumors, the wide-spread suspicion of a new Man-God abroad and walking the street, had even at moments thought it might be himself.) At that moment the sun dropped abruptly behind the wall; Lee could see a cadre of black people emptying out hurriedly from one of the doorways and scattering in all directions. Nothing surprised him anymore. He saw an expensive car from the outside world, lights dimmed, searching for something.

He found himself peering in at the pawnshop, a most narrow establishment and so loaded with curiosities that there was hardly room for the grinning eminence within. They looked at each other. Lee had seen him before, in Detroit or somewhere, and always with the same display of gangrenous watches and musical instruments. He saw a photograph album open to a well-dressed family, now all extinct. Lee focused on the family dog, its expression showing the aftereffects of a joke that had recently taken place. It too, extinct. Next, his eye fell upon a knife with a devilishly long blade, long enough for piercing even to the deepest of organs. He had said there were no bookstores in Alabama, yet here was a set of something or another, twenty volumes in brown vellum; it put him in mind of his own beloved collection now wasting in the arms of the Law.

He turned, almost colliding with the eminence who had come outside and was standing, arms behind his back.

"Lovely evening."

"Cold, though."

"We have men's coats."

"No, no. I was looking at the books."

"Oh, Updike; yes he was read at one time. We have shoes."

"No, no; I have a better pair at . . ." (He had started to say "home.")

"And walking canes; we have some very fine ones."

"Ah. But do you have *heavy* ones?"

"Oh yes, absolutely."

"Heavier than *this*? Knob on top?"

The man took it and looked it over thoughtfully. It occurred to Lee that he had let it go too easily, that possibly it was a ruse of some kind.

"Where did you get this cane?"

"Detroit." (They looked at each other.)

"It's already very heavy."

"I know."

"I wouldn't have anything heavier."

"I see."

"We have small arms."

"No, no. Do you have mattresses?"

"No mattresses. Pharmaceuticals we have."

"If I could just have my cane now . . ."

"Nazi regalia?"

"No, no." He had to fight for it; the man was strong. Lee's plan was to stamp on the foot, which was large and covered much pavement; instead, the cane fell free at the last moment.

"Interrogation equipment?"

"No, no, no." He hurried away, past a deserted place and next, a grocery doing big business in spite of the hour. He had a stark view of women who, all thoughts of romance now put to one side, were going about the more serious business of getting the best of the fruits and vegetables. Next, to his surprise, was a private home with gate and garden and little old woman on the porch summoning him to come up and sit a while. Lee hurried on, coming next upon an antique shop so quaint and picturesque . . . He knew them. Hardly had he stepped inside before a girl came up with a warm and patronizing smile, as if she knew all his secrets and found them quaint as well. To be deemed harmless—nothing riled him more, nothing easier than to impale her with his cane.

"Hi!"

"Mattresses."

She had none. She did have a way of smiling that let him see the quality of her fillings. Seldom had he come across so exquisite a sample of the shallowness revolution; moreover, every step he took forward, she took one back! She seemed to be made out of a pearly material, such as would fly apart at the first touch of a cane.

"You ever read a book in your life? No."

She was smiling no more. Now it was fear he smelled, astringent stuff, stronger by far than perfume.

"I'll scream."

"Do so! Myself, I've done nothing as yet."

"You can have the money, I won't even say anything. No, really!"

"Money?" He showed his money. "It's not money."

"I'm having my period."

"Keep it! No, all I want from you is one intelligent word. Just one! You can't, can you?" He counted, even to ten. "Very well, do this—just *look* serious. Oh, I'll give you plenty of time!" Indeed, he even backed up a step or two. Behind him, he could hear slop music in loudness from one of the cars. The girl herself was striving earnestly, but with no real hope of forcing her expression into anything he could let pass.

"I didn't say you couldn't breathe."

"Can I stop?"

"No, you can't stop! Not till you're rid of that 'pearly' look."

That moment someone entered and, seeing that something was happening, stood still. It never failed, never: each time he felt he was making progress, some third party always burst into his life. This time it was a well-dressed woman in middle-age, rather portly, with shopping bags and purse. Lee summoned her around and next to the girl, somewhat appeased in that she obeyed so quickly.

"What about you, you know anything? Don't look at her, look at me. *She* doesn't know anything."

It was interesting—the fat one appeared to have some little fund of knowledge and appeared actually to be searching in it. The other was weeping.

"Ready? Alright, name me all those whom Achilles slew."

"'Slew.'" She *was* thinking. Against all odds, he found himself cheering for her.

"Horace? No, wait. Hadrian? No. Oh, Homer! Herodotus? Herodian? No, cancel that last. Hold! I have it—Hector!"

Lee grinned; it was a good moment. Hardly ever had he felt so proud of anyone. His hand on the cane relaxed, away from the girth of it.

"See? Now, that's better! Very well, you can go. No,

I mean it! And take anything you want, too. Those necklaces? Take 'em all!"

She was coy about it; finally, she did take one, and then, going to the door and coming back, three more. He heard the special sound of a fat woman galloping off on concrete. As for the girl, she was sniveling still. It was not so much the desire to cane her as to instill her with fiber enough that she might at least stand up straight.

"It's a great mistake to count over much on my patience. Now hear me: I'm coming back someday, maybe a year, maybe tomorrow, and you had best *know* something at that time. Now, is that fair?"

She nodded, sniveling. Again he showed the cane, the blunt part. For himself, the shop had nothing he wanted, unless it were certain old movie posters that he couldn't use. He remembered backtracking, till he was out the door and around to the window, where he waited a long while, watching still.

Night always, if he had his way. In front of the shops two men had pulled a third out of a car and were beating him very quietly. Here, in the "canyon" (so-called), Lee liked to pause and gaze straight up, sometimes catching a faraway face peering straight down. There was smoke, a playful stuff, that flooded his shoes. All in all he would have said the slum was green in the moon and blue in the shade, while the voices that came to him were so distorted, as if people everywhere were gagged and screaming with mouths sewed up tight. More than ever at this hour the buildings looked like cow pats piled tidily; he could have punched round holes in them with his cane.

He climbed the stairs, past the chaos of the second floor and thence to his own landing. There was a bar of light beneath one of the doors and a shadow where someone was standing. It gave him a wonderful feeling to be in his own room, naked as it might indeed be, and with bad smells. Someone had died here recently; it infected even the corners.

It was not a good moment for him. He could see across town to the very building where even now the authorities were swarming over his books. He could not bring forth Judy into *this*, nor allow her to see how he was living. Suddenly, the dread flooded over him that he had perhaps locked himself away for the night without matches. Quickly, he unpacked the money, also the tiny volume of Musæus that he had forgotten about. There *were* matches, a box of little yellow-tipped devils of Swedish manufacture; he struck one, then blew it out. Somewhere a radio was playing. It was not so early that he was the only person in the slum wanting sleep. His habit was to fabricate a dream in advance and then insist upon having it, but not tonight, not without books. Outside, a cloud was dissolving in a kind of tedious slowness, like cloth to shreds; perhaps he was asleep already.

It took two matches; she came to him in beauty at one of his favorite ages. He ought have known she wouldn't mind about the room, not when she had never minded such things in reality. Right away he took her to bed and lay holding her about the back.

"Look at that sky!"

"I know."

Now he could sleep, it was easy *now*.

Sixteen

HAVING WOKEN LATE, RISEN, and walked about the room, he got back in bed. Down below a commotion had broken out—Jebuzites haggling among the booths. All morning he had been lying abed, struggling to turn into a spiritual entity while down below everyone was devoted to the *body* and its things. Let them rather be, if not artists and intellectuals, then heroes at least, and if not heroes, artists then, or intellectuals. In fact, nothing would satisfy him better than to sleep through these next fifty years, and then wake into a bright yellow day with fine people and a new religion once again giving the sun its reverence. Deep was his hatred for the modern age, so deep and so rich, a rich feast. How he envied the times to come, the world made clear.

Now he was sleeping, but so lightly that he was able, as it were, to monitor the process. Someone was in the hall; he could hear it. Now he dreamed of that young man of the future that he himself was to have been, were it the future and were he young. But most of all, it was the knowledge of all the days and hours that still lay in front of him, together with the certainty that any moment now he would be encountering his wife for the first time again, the ten millionth time he had done so.

A line of gray-colored cars was seething out of town—it made him wonder if they might know something that he did not. By his reckoning it should have been dark two hours ago and everyone locked away in their stalls. This was the bad time, with a long dead space between now and nightfall; to his knowledge, nothing in history had ever taken place this time of day. Nevertheless, he went back and lay face down, counting, quite prepared to wait howsoever long it might take.

He was sleeping, peacefully too (floating in cream), when his soul became dislodged and began to slip free. Nothing could have prepared him for what followed. He had had some peculiar sensations in his time—faintings, hemorrhoids, orgasmics, etc., etc., etc.—but nothing on *this* scale. Heretofore, he had thought of the soul as small, a Japanese machine, instead, it was nearly the size of a doll and with a horrid little head on it. Moreover, once under way, he found that he could no more have halted the process than . . .

It was the blunt end came first. Somewhere he had read of how the fetus recapitulates the history of the beast, whereas in this case, the face was all innocence and awe and—this surprised him—sucking its thumb. He was being offered a chance that would soon expire: to remain with body and die, or take the risk of leaping aboard the soul and fly.

There was no fear; he had done his fearing during the seventy-two years. Now came the light fixture (or he to it), nor did it seem to him in the least strange that he was floating under the ceiling in a state of calm, which fled away, however, very quickly when he saw that he could see through walls. First, he saw a woman, two floors down, sitting on the toilet. Directly beneath him, of course, lay his own untenanted body—a long one, and with a face (and this *really* surprised him) that must have looked entirely ordinary to anyone who didn't know him better. It had always seemed to him monstrous to have taken up in human form anyway, a vile manifestation with poor endurance and with beauty that was well below average for the animal kind. Moreover, he had worn it out completely, misused it so . . . He was glad his mother couldn't see it. Suddenly he felt sleepy.

The body was still there, wrinkling under his eyes. As for himself, he was beginning to feel somewhat cramped. Again he pushed off, sailing over the body. It was all so new; he thought about his money. Nor could he understand why he was getting no help. Judy! Why had she not flown to his side?

His anxiety increased. Once he had imagined this would be his chance to see the lost books of Theopompos of Chios perhaps, not simply to float forever in a hotel room that was airless. He found himself humming, then, dredging up pictures from Herodotus. It embittered him: how he had had thus to pass through the "keyhole" of death simply to get back into times (small population of fine people) that were proper for a person of his kind; indeed, he almost felt sorry for those others, now also dead, who had never studied and therefore knew not how to use such a toy. Again he pushed off. All his life he had wanted to spend one evening in Ionic antiquity or, better still, go walking with his wife in the lovely swirling Silurian, by far the most gorgeous of ages. He could see it: two of them watching silently on shore at great comets flinging past. Instead, he woke—woke, called and fell, and found himself in the corpse once more.

Seventeen

THIS SLUM HAD A MEMBRANE; sidling to the opening, Lee tested it with the cane. The sentry was a slovenly man, always marching back and forth in what looked to be a hat of tin and with what appeared to be a musket; Lee had to clap hand over mouth to keep from bursting into mirth. And yet the gate was an easy matter to get open, a mere common latch of the household type.

He could identify these middle-class neighborhoods by the size of their television sets and whether the children had actual pajamas or went to bed in underwear; at once, he veered off the walk and up to the nearest window. It was a domestic scene; one might almost have thought it the 1950's again, save for people's faces. It was a strange truth—greater the possessions, littler the possessors. *He* recommended a life of near-poverty and time for long walks; what he *saw* was a man and wife still in business clothes and three little rotten children with, each of them, billions of complaints. He came nearer, shielding his eyes, only at the last minute giving himself away by the sound of his glasses clicking on the pane.

He knew these people—they daren't come out after him *themselves*. Instead, he cut across, down someone's yard and into a mown place where a good-size dog came bounding up in delight. There was a ditch and then a culvert, put there expressly for him to hide in. Here he smoked, wasting time. At one point he almost fell off to sleep. Only the dog could have revealed his location, and the dog had gone off bored.

It was near to two in the morning before he came out and, at first, lurched off in the wrong direction. He could see the moon, once his own special star, also the gigantic silhouette of the towering apartment complex known as "Nietzsche's Head." Then Lee recognized a home with high-peaked roof where a friend of his once had dwelt. He craved to rush inside, rouse the man, and see whether he still had any playfulness left (having once been famous for it); instead, he settled for gathering up two small stones and tossing them to the second-story window.

He loved these late night walks; never in his day had he been permitted out at this time, no doubt because the beauty had been too much for his young frame. Now that it was beautiful indeed, the mature people chose to be asleep! He would never understand it. Sometimes his contempt boiled over into a kind of spittle. The neighborhood was tidy, yes, but paid for by extreme simplification of mind. Now Lee pissed, but not into the grass; there was a rich little car with the window down.

The next house had been destroyed, burnt two months ago, and already there was a new foundation in place. He might burn one each hour, it didn't matter; their number were without end.

He pushed on, into darker homes and lower ground. One house was perfect—a brown object with turfen roof. Someone here was awake, awake and reading behind a window that was itself made of little bookish squares. He could not help but go and press against it with his ear. He heard numerous things: a clock, a page being turned. Apparently, he had here someone in the perfect house reading the perfect book. And music! this too perfect, courtesy of Ravel; ten seconds of it and Lee was back in Hellas. He pleaded it to go on forever; instead, it stopped. He could feel his gorge rise. He might or might not have been able to jab through the window, perhaps or perhaps not catching the reader in the eye or temple. And as always with people that he couldn't actually see, there was always the infinitesimal chance that it might be a fine person.

He came away sadly. Another fifty yards and he was back in typical houses, white ones with no trees about and nothing good inside. He could pinpoint the decline in history—when the uneducated are given comfortable houses. He saw a stained-glass window-portrait of a certain famous football coach rendered to look like Jesus.

It was now three in the morning, for him the second-best time in the day. The moon was weak, however, and looked like a quoit. Somewhere here he had had his first aesthetic experience once, now so many years ago that he couldn't remember what had brought it on. It had ruined him, he knew *that.* Suddenly, that instant, he saw something—a wolf, or mayhap a jackal—flashing out of the woods. They looked at each other. *Now* Lee remembered what had caused his experience so long ago.

* * *

He had to spend a good long time on the lock. Then he went past the "tea room" and up the stairs. He weighed almost nothing these days, and yet each step yelped out loud and clear. He half expected a barrier around his room, even a lout standing guard in uniform, but there was nothing of the kind. Again, they had underrated him, not even so much as switching keys on him!

A minute went by while he stood in darkness. His books were all around, hundreds gasping at his audacious return. He had forgotten the comforts of the place, the carpet. Perhaps he could take up residence again! No, not likely, not with policemen coming back ever and anon to finish off the Schopenhauer. Instead, Lee stripped off the pillowcase; then, working in the dark by touch alone, he began to fill the bag. This was that dilemma he had always dreaded—that of having to choose which of the world's writings to salvage and which let lapse. Murray's *Homer*—he cared nothing for his country but would have laid down his life for Murray's *Homer*—two copies. Hesiod certainly, Herodotus too. True, he had some modern books, also hermit literature of the greater Western anchorites, and yet, when all was over, the bag near to bursting, everything he kept had come from Greece.

Few things are more pleasant than to break into middle-class territory and take what one wants, and break out again. Outside, he began whistling. This was that same route as when he used to be off to school with his pencils and child books—he could feel himself grow tender at thought of it. He had been good from the beginning, a thinking man from the time he was three, and all of it in a country that hated such things. Suddenly, he broke out laughing, a ringing sound that caused him to put down his bag first and then, as it got worse, to try and stifle the coughing. He rather wished these occupants *would* come out and see what he was thinking. No doubt about it, his hatred was increasing, his wisdom too; he now looked upon himself as the century's most preeminent prophet of the coming of the cracking of the West. Heads he saw, heads for reaping, eyes, buckets of eyes. His job was to spend as much time as he still had in becoming as hard as he still could, exhilarating as it most certainly was.

He slipped into the slum, past the watchman fast asleep, thence to his favorite all-night tavern called The Pied Cow. First, he saw a drunk by the fireplace looking jealously at his bag. Lee went straight to his place, but then leaped back when he found it occupied already. In the end, he had to sit at a small table, his back exposed. Moreover, on top of that, the waitress was so exhausted and dilatory he had time to open the bag and, as it were, *stir* in it somewhat. And when she did come, it was to bring a plate of beans with all the color gone and two wan dollops of prechewed meat. He noticed how all things here had a film of grease, a slippery deposit good for writing messages in; twice his elbow flew out from under him.

It was necessary to be grateful for the small things—namely, that there were no young people about, no "music." In back, he could spot the cook, an emaciated man looking around in some indignation at the quality of the customers. Lee himself was bending, very nearly asleep, when an elderly man came up of a sudden and, as if the table were not already crowded enough, took the place opposite. Lee stood, then sat down again.

"Yes?"

"I saw you over here. Thinking, right? You know, it's not often I run into someone *our* age, not here at the 'Cow' leastwise."

Our age! In fact the man was old and had a cane. Lee looked at him coldly. "I'll be leaving in a moment."

"Take your time! it don't bother me. Don't have any tobacco, do you?"

One more hour and the sun would have been up; Lee had looked forward to it, the display. Now, instead, he had been delivered over unto an acidic-looking old man who kept poking the bag with his cane.

"What you got in there, money?" He laughed.

"No, no, I keep that in my coat."

"Indeed!"

Lee showed it to him, then tried to go back to reading.

"My lands, you need to *invest* that stuff!! Unless of course you want some of these niggers around here to take it."

"No, no—that's *usury*. Besides, I always take *this*." (He showed the cane.)

"Why lands, that's not going to do you any good! Why they've got *knives* longer than that. 'Usury!'"

"But do they know how to *use* them? Knives, I mean."

"Shore they do! I *know*."

"But I'm talking *speed*, man; do they have the *speed*?" (Suddenly Lee stood and thrashed wildly once or twice, showing his speed. It was a mistake, of course; instead of departing, the man was getting more and more interested.)

"I don't know. When I look at you . . ."

Lee hummed, then took out the Musæus. The man's eyes were weak and red; moreover, he kept leaning across the table in order to see more clearly.

"Knew it!" the other said finally. "By God, I knew it. As soon as I set eyes on you: 'That ole boy over there,' I said (speaking to myself, you understand), 'that old boy over there, he just don't give a shit about nothing.' Was I right?"

"Look, why don't you just finish up that 'ale,' if that's what it can properly be called. The sun's going to be up very shortly now."

"Come around here with your little goddamn sack of money. Maybe you don't even belong here! Anyway, *I've* never seen you before."

Lee sighed, but then finally said it out loud: "Oh, you've seen him alright, indeed you have. Miss Hatcher's third grade?"

The man's mouth flew open. "*You* were that little shit?"

"Oh, yes."

"All the time with that little goddamn clarinet?"

"Absolutely."

"Well I'll be jiggered. Say, you don't seem to have made out too well, do you?"

"Oh? Where's *your* little sack of money?"

"You know something, I'll tell you the solemn truth: you're nothing in this world but *trash*—I hate to say that to a man of your age."

Lee grinned.

"Smile then, do! I reckon you don't care about nothing—not me, not the *Cow*, and not the country neither!"

"It's finished."

"What's that I hear you say?"

"Finished. Oh, I don't say it won't slop along for another two or three hundred years."

"Why . . . my God . . . you're a bad man!"

Lee grinned. "You realize, of course, that you have a tic right . . ."—he touched the spot—"there! Right under the left eye."

"That's right, keep it up, I know your type. Why

boy, I've been handling your type all my life! It's not your country you hate, but . . ."

Lee stood.

". . . life. That's right! And now if you ain't too grand to step outside . . ."

"By all means."

"I'm going to whup you good, boy."

"With *my* speed? In fact, you're going to wish you were back in the third grade."

"Fourth."

"Third, I'm telling you."

"Debra Mae? I reckon you remember *her*, don't you?"

He was right. Lee could see her even now, a dark-complected girl. It was the man grinning now, a most obscene smile. Lee yelled at him.

"Blackguard!" Then: "*Had* to screw her, didn't you? Hound. You know, I hadn't really intended to kill you, but I shall certainly do so now. I've killed four already, you should know."

"*You* the one doing all that?"

They rose and filed out, the cook coming too. There was a blank wall on the other side, enough to fence them in and keep the other from running away. One thing did trouble him: he had never before had to do with someone of his own generation, formidable and, like himself, with nothing to lose.

"Very well, and now I shall hove your skull in."

They engaged. Lee was hardened to the sound of cane on bone followed by shrieks; this time it was clashing sticks. He didn't like it. The man was *good*, especially with cross strokes and parry. Lee aimed one at his fibula, but almost fell himself. Now for the first time he saw the full horror of it, to be set upon by an old man with large weapon. He didn't like it.

"Freemason!"

Suddenly, Lee took one to the crown—painful. No one had ever treated him this way. He goggled, eyes bulging, then brought down his own stick with such force that it made a chiming sound. He was in peril of losing this battle. He wanted his hat, a helmet, umbrella or book, anything to save his head. Came now another strike straight to his neck, formerly his own special target. Now that he thought about it, the other man was perhaps a few months younger than himself and, moreover, had passed his entire life in the cruel South. Suddenly, Lee nicked the man's Adam's apple.

"Hey! You hit me right in the throat!"

"Yes, and I'm going after the nose next."

And he did so, a well-targeted strike that made the sort of noise Lee was addicted to. Now the man had two wounds, both bleeding; moreover, his cane was bent. He never saw Lee's foot (shaped like a trowel), surprisingly swift as it was. The man called once (to Lee it sounded like an owl), then went down. Lee's heart sang—until the man tackled and brought him down as well. He had a terrible vision of money running out of his pocket and bills lying in view. It was a choice of gathering them up again or pounding on the man.

He would have preferred to be in bed; instead, the man bore down again upon him with his cane, shortened as it now was. The sun had come up three minutes ago in great splendor, but Lee could not enjoy it. He parried. He was himself bleeding from the head and seemed to have snapped his finger again. His friend was clearly having the worst of it, and yet (Lee admitted it), he never once called for help. He even experienced a certain grudging sympathy for all such boys as had grown up in the same town and never gone away. Suddenly, seeing an opening, he came down mightily on that same nose as was already in such a state.

"Had enough?"

"No, no." (But it was the cook that said it.)

"What time is it?"

"I don't know. Sun's up."

"How about that nose?"

"Leave it alone.

"Are you sorry now about all the things you've done?"

"Yes, yes. I don't want to hear no more about it."

"And Debra?"

"Yes, yes, yes. You have to understand: it was *her* idea." They glared, and then, suddenly, the other turned on his heel and strode away. Lee shook his cane at him, one last insult before sprinting back to the café where already the new day's breakfast clientele was making a great noise. It was about what he had expected: the drunk had taken his books, and when he came back, the cook had taken his bills.

Eighteen

FOUR TIMES HE WENT TO THE WINdow, his exasperation growing. He had swollen places on his crown, the beginning of horns. His glasses were broken. He wanted it dark, wanted silence, wanted the working people to drop their tools and go back into their cells again. Nothing so infuriated him as this continual ripping up and laying down of pavement and road, as if that way happiness might be found. He liked woods.

By four the slum was dark; by six, the world. Waiting by the window, he could mark the very moment it changed from day to night. Two minutes ago it was all pragmatical people scurrying home with worried faces; now suddenly, he saw youths emptying out into the street in bright colors. He saw a large woman in a tight skirt; behind her, a mere adolescent trailed along with a face sick from lust and too much neon. Across the way was an open window—it looked like a picture tacked up in space—revealing a woman ironing and a depressed-looking man sitting on the bed. This was twentieth-century stuff, another five thousand years before civilization could have its start, and yet, even where he was going, he knew he'd miss it someday. Either he would mix into the sun or, according to another of his theories, pay for his errors with a long-term stint as a one-celled thing.

He rolled, groaned, dressed, urinated, and hummed. There were at least four persons next door—he could hear them coming awake one by one and then hastening to get into their colorful clothes. Saturday! He wanted to puke. It was then he noticed that the radio tower was flashing in a crisis, having changed from red to purple.

He waited by the door and then, suddenly, burst out in great leap so as to foil anyone who might be lying in wait. He saw all manner of black people waiting to go outside, yet who were reluctant to do so. Lee went half a block, then he stopped to watch the daytime police withdrawing slowly in a group, step by step, finally snapping the gate shut behind them. He then saw something that chilled him to the soul—a huge man with his head shaved down the middle in the Lombard style described by Gibbon. The other direction held a crowd of youths, a grinning species that made Lee's gorge rise to look at them. Under the circumstances, he hardly knew what to do. Nor was he willing to go upstairs again, not with "music" above and "music" below and "music" in the hall.

Instead, he lit a cigarette. The storefront had a niche—Lee was ten feet deep in it before he espied a second party there, a girl it looked, who had huddled up at the back, watching him steadily in fear. Twenty years ago and he might have offered aid, but not now, not when he actually took satisfaction in things going from bad to worse. Just then a man strode past, one of the last of the good ones hastening home before too late. Lee immediately came hobbling out after him with noise and goggling eye; he did so love to see these types run, especially the pudgy ones leaving trails of cologne.

He came back, laughing, and again squeezed into the cave. The girl had come forward, drugged apparently.

"Still here? Out, out, out!"

No answer. She seemed not to hear.

"What is it—cold?"

"Yeah."

"Well. Socrates used to do some of his best thinking in the cold. Now if *he* could stay out all night in the snow, then *you* . . ."

"Want to fuck?"

"What! What! I'm *old*, can't you see that?"

"Want to look at it?"

"No I don't want to look at it! Jove!"

"Got five dollars?"

"Certainly."

"Lend it to me, okay?"

"Certainly not." He went closer. This one had dead eyes, and her mouth hung open; there were other symptoms too that related to the quantity of television and advertisements in her head. "Television! Alright, out, out, out!"

He had to hiss and raise the stick up high. Finally she did break past and through the opening and—he could scarce believe it—straight into the arms of the Lombard across the road!

He wasted half an hour, sometimes coming out from the niche and exploring for a block or two. The moon was large, and kept him too stirred-up for his bleak room, where nothing would be happening just now. A taxi came. Lee waited until the client had paid his fare before leaping on board himself. He would have preferred an older driver, one who had done all and seen all and knew to obey without showing too much surprise.

"I should like to run out into the country for a spell—can you do that?"

"Country."

"Yes. Why must you repeat it? And try to find me a scene like . . . I don't know . . . sixteenth century perhaps!"

The car did not budge; moreover, the man was watching in the mirror. Lee expected it. Finally, he took out the money and showed it in one hand and the cane in the other.

It looked more to him like Akkad, with its clay villages and squat little tombs of the "beehive" style, all of it exactly as when the original inhabitants had run off and left it. The moon too, also made of clay, was so much without shape it looked as if someone had been kneading with it. What he wanted now was music, music and Judy, music, Judy, and a ship that would steer itself. Further, he had determined that if the driver once more glanced in the mirror, it would be so much the worse for his head, which was already rather nonsymmetrical. Finally, three miles out, he took out the matches.

She materialized immediately. Tonight she was sparkling, grinning, and dressed out in a blue suit that was itself very like the night. He knew so little about the place whence she came.

"Judy, Judy."

"I'm here."

It was this woman's voice (deep for one so short) that caused the man to veer suddenly and almost go off into the woods.

"Just keep your goddamn eyes on the goddamn road!"

A windmill came up, with what looked to him to be a hanged man dangling from the paddles. He had seen this before in books—the sixteenth century and certain bloody wars of the Dutch. He saw a starved mule, and next, a house on fire and some tens of crazed soldiers dancing joyously with heads on pikes.

"You see?" (It was Judy.) "It's always been bad. Had you rather be back in those days?"

"I suppose not."

"No."

"What is it—Thirty Years' War?"

"No, this one didn't even get written about."

That instant a barn went up in an explosion of bright beautiful flame.

"It's Greece you want, isn't it?"

"Judy! Is it possible?" He stared, running over suddenly with amazement, fear, alarm. "It can't be done."

"Oh?"

"No! Let's not, Judy."

"You might not like it."

"I know, I know."

She was laughing, still teasing after all these years; she had a method for being eighteen and fifty at the same time. Suddenly:

"I *told* you to keep your goddamn eyes on that road!" He lifted the cane; Judy pressed it down again.

They had come into high country now, the Zagros chain, as it seemed to him. Here the huts were miserable and, apart from goats, he could see no livestock anywhere. He had seen better than this in Alabama. Indeed, he questioned whether all things had not already long ago happened in one fell moment of wildest doing. Or rather, that there was no Time, no millions, no history, but only one giant monster with infinite fingers and eyes without count.

"No such thing as 'Time,' right?"

She looked at him in surprise; nothing made him more proud than to come up with these discoveries of his ever and again, based upon his wisdom and reading.

"Very well, I think I'd like to see Greece now. But not 'straight on,' as it were—too risky—might blind me. No, could I just see Lycia instead? Till you count to ten?"

"Lycia!" She laughed merrily. "There 'tis! I'm counting."

It was fine. Not that Grecian Greece of the Greeks, to be sure, but the epoch was right. The people—rather small-seeming, to his eyes.

"What are they *thinking*?"

"You always ask that." She laughed, then that same moment his time ran out. Amazingly, they were back in Alabama, viewing an undistinguished landscape with litter and a people whom he knew from personal experience to be below the norm. He saw a man in a tiny cabin with a huge television. The very shape of his ears and head revealed everything one needed to know about his spiritual state.

"Look at that one."

In fact, she had gone. He fumbled desperately for the matches, dropped them, then came up to find the driver's vile face searching in the mirror.

"Goddamn it! I *told* you . . ."

"Alright, mister, that's all for you."

Indeed, they slowed, then actually stopped; Lee found himself looking down into a valley that was not at all like that of Xanthus. Hurriedly he showed his money.

"That won't do you no good."

"*This* will." He showed the cane.

"Nope."

Now Lee saw the man had a pistol—and was showing it.

It was disappointing in the real air, with real stones under foot—a much smaller experience than dreaming about it aboard a cab. *Then* he was warm; now, cold. Probably it was a mistake to have left the highway, all of it from his unwillingness to meet up with another traveler possibly, or police, and then having to explain himself.

He liked to steer by the moon, now once more his own special star. Tonight the thing was but three-fourths full and yet already greater than the Peloponnese; he could see a long flight of yellow crows weaving homeward to it in drunkenness. Below lay a village, vacant these hundred years and yet still giving off smoke. The woods were dense with animals, a naïve population that had been pushed back into the dark corners, never knowing why. As for himself, he would prefer to see a thousand men disemboweled than one more lizard with a missing tail. Based upon what he knew about the anti-world, it were better to be disemboweled one's self than to have murdered even one.

By the time he hit town, he was loaded down with flowers, no two of them the same. He stopped. He had seen the sun in splendor, he had never seen it like *this*—rose-colored wafer with idiots dancing on the rim. Someday, he knew it, the beauty of things would break him where he stood.

According to his theory, he could go on developing for as long as he disbelieved everything the modern age promoted. Mostly, he disbelieved that this "bloodsun" was not the deity that he could right well see that, in fact, it was. His instinct was to get him down on both knees in praise; instead, he turned into a driveway, a garden, a good place to pee and have a cigarette.

He had slept! Sleeping in the city! He knew it from the first instant the man's shoe nudged him in the ribs. At once Lee leapt up, but then he had to grab hold of the individual to keep from falling.

"What's going on here!"

"Ha! Nothing. Or very little anyway." He laughed. "All's well as seems well!" Again he laughed, slapping the man in friendly-wise.

"Are you ill?"

"Ha! No, no. No, I was just . . ."

They looked at each other. It was simply a man, no better or worse than others of the kind. Lee saw at least three places—hip, thigh, and pot—where he was available to attack.

"Do you need a doctor?"

"Doctor! No, no—you know how squeamish *they* are. So!" Suddenly he turned and strode off. The man's wife had retreated into her home where he could very definitely see her in consternation behind glass. Ahead, two miles further, was his own hotel, six royal pennants fluttering gaily in the breeze.

Nineteen

DAYS PASSED. SO SILENT WAS IT, time so slow . . . Heretofore he had needed books on one side and music on the other; now it was the sun alone, hours upon hours of it while he stared, wide-eyed, in a four-floor hotel. Some numbers of insects had penetrated the room; he spied them here and there, looking back with that unblinking eagerness he so much hated to see. Never leaving the bed, he was thinking more deeply than most people would have believed possible. Other times, he would lie on one side for long periods, praying no one would burst in upon him in his condition. He might move one hand slightly, he was very far from being able to grasp the cane. These were not moments so much as entire days going by, the wallpaper deteriorating even as he watched. He could feel his time approaching, the great noontide.

In Alabama some winter days are like spring. *Then* would Lee bound up and stick his head out, as if he imagined it were childhood and his own most memorable dog were somersaulting for him to come out again and play. Instead, finding it winter, Lee drew back in. He had doubts he would see many more summers, summers that is as summers are commonly understood. Or, that he ever again would run with his dog in earthly shape. Nothing could be more tantalizing than this persisting hunger, old as he was, for music, dogs, Judy, and milk-white pages. He wanted to live, wanted to die, wanted a final reckoning with all who had wronged him.

One day he got up and shaved and then went back to bed again. Finally, a Thursday, he threw himself out into the hall and thence to the lobby, where a new-age woman in foot-long earbobs was sitting in haughty array. For five seconds Lee stood, counting. Her neck was so thin, her nature such, she could have no slightest suspicion as to how near she was to a very grim death. His hand twitched once, then relaxed from the cane.

He went out. It was one of those listless afternoons, as when a great man has recently died. For himself, he was beginning to question whether he was still visible or not—no one paid notice to him—and whether there might not be yet older people who had turned completely invisible. Suddenly it came to him that he had not tasted of food in days.

He ran, past one restaurant that was full and then on to another that was so dark and evil-smelling that no one attended anymore. Lee saw the chef, a haunted man with arms dipped in gore. According to Lee's expectation, the waitress must needs be a widow and grandmother, slow-moving, tired, washed-out and with bad feet, wanting nothing, poor and hardly able to remember any longer the farmstead where she had grown up—he saw her in the corner. This was most definitely *his* class of restaurant, here where he had space and dimness and no requirement to be within seeing distance of rotten youths. He searched the place, finally settling for a stagnant booth at the rear from which he could study the street, but the street could not study him.

First, a woman, old and forlorn—he had seen her so many times: fifty years ago in Toledo, in Chicago had he seen her, Iowa, Ohio and France. By now he could even put himself in her head and look out through her eyes, and what he saw were children and grandchildren scattered to the winds. Another strange thing: Formerly, he had detested the old and admired what was young; now, it was the other way around, and in a country that adored movement and noise.

The waitress brought his fare, more paste-colored slum slop made of dextrin and hoof mucilage. She was mournful, this one—he divined that her children had not scattered merely, but expired. And had she not one time been pretty perhaps, and had he not himself once chased her screaming into a closet and kissed her while she fought? He was almost certain that he had not.

This day his stomach wanted nothing in it, not even a swig of milk. Nevertheless, Lee tossed the stuff in and sucked on it. To his mind, eating was obscene at the best of times, but so long indulged-in that no one any longer recognized it for what it was. Suddenly, half-asleep as he was, he spotted a couple that snapped him out of his stupor and sent him chasing out onto the street. Something in their faces—these were the first unspoilt people he had seen in fourteen years. Holding hands too! His mind flew back to the 1950's when he had personally known any number of such types, unbesmirched ones, and in a country with a structure to it.

He put on speed. Indeed, this was a girl (high forehead, bouncing hair) worth fighting for, dying for if one couldn't have her, and yes, the world had once been full of such people. However, she was taking far too much pleasure in her swain and the sun on her forehead to listen to any warnings of *his*; instead, he let himself fall in behind.

He followed halfway across the slum, weaving in and out, sometimes walking abreast, till at last they seemed to grow accustomed to it. They were young, yet not so very young as not to have been doing things these recent weeks. Indeed, he saw them whispering about it jubilantly. Lee groaned. She did have the most good lips, swollen with yearning. Mettlesome was she too, and had a dear white hand swinging back and forth, which he durst not take, however.

He remembered the three of them entering a store, then of waiting around while she selected a ribbon for herself. She looked good in this. She knew it, Lee knew it, and the boy knew it too. Next, they returned to the street again and made the brief walk to the gate. He had thought to see a parting here, instead they both ducked out through the shaft and appeared on the other side. It was here they decided to kiss. Lee groaned. Her blue eye was half-closed, and yet he could read enough in it to recall what it was to hold a woman in one's arms. Lee came nearer; he had his way, and the boy would hold more tightly still, lest she worm out of his grasp and run away. Suddenly, he called out:

"Careful!"

They kissed. Perhaps if he studied closely enough in that blue eye, he might read the date of her death, the names and numbers of her offspring, or better, the look of the world in thirty years to come. Again they came together, this time so frantically, with so much true feeling, that Lee moaned and howled and called—and ended up cudgeling on the sentry!

Twenty

YEARS PASSED—OR RATHER A FEW days in which he was able to conjure up in his mind exactly what such years would bring. He didn't want it. In any case, his health and money both were running low. This was not at all the grand species he had been led to believe, and he had no ten million years for the next one to come on board.

Often he would rise early, but then go back to bed. Contrary to everything, he had actually come to appreciate his room, its bleakness, and the hotel, too, which seemed now abandoned, since even the jester had gone away. Then too, the view from his window gave him some happiness—he liked to sit there long hours with his wife, pointing to peasants in the field and events that had happened in history.

He did grieve for his books, even if he wasn't so sure he had a vocation for them anymore. Instead, he was drawn again and again to the window and the scenery that more and more was coming to serve as his own special manuscript, an example of the printmaker's art, with cottages and exuberant swine walking around. Once only he caught sight of that new-made sun, huger by far and more brilliant, heralding a new sort of man; for one instant, it peeped up over the horizon and then ducked back down.

First, there would be an end to cities. *He'd* not see it, no, nor receive credit for having laid out the actual plans for what was coming up next—small world of fine people. Last year, he had wanted a thousand acres for each living soul; now, he had moved on to fifteen hundred and a spiritual system that . . . Suddenly, he heard something on one of the floors, a most untowardly sound that put him on guard at once and had him considering whether to slip beneath the bed. Though he was often mistaken about many things, he had never yet been mistaken when hostile forces were coming close. Officially speaking, the hotel was empty, but now he could most definitely hear at least two persons, large ones blundering about ignorantly in the style of the Law. His own pistol was lost; moreover, to make matters worse, his bed was so high it gave a view upon anyone hoping to hide beneath. He hurried out into the hall and then upstairs to an apartment where a large family had formerly lived. Here the bed was low. He got under it.

It all took such a time that he almost fell off to sleep. Now he could hear them rooting about in his room while giving off little squeals of joy. Recently, he had put aside a hoard of tobacco and canned foods and the like; now (he had no doubt), this too was forfeit.

He held his breath, waiting for the inevitable departure; instead, he heard them trooping up the stairs, heard them conferring, heard a knocking at the door. From his hiding place he could see a rubberized sole that, owing no doubt to the size and substance of the person, was squeezed down to an amazing thinness. Lee didn't like it. This was *not* how he had foreseen it when he was young and used to hypothesize how his personal tragedy might turn out.

There was now a large red face, a balloon really, grinning at him in the sideways position.

"Oh lookie, I think I sees something. I do, I do sees something!"

Lee might have knocked out both eyes with his cane; instead, he retreated. He fully expected to be dragged out into the light. He expected it so much that he knew not what to say when, in fact, they simply lifted the bed and moved it a far distance away. He scampered for it, ardent to return under its shade, until he recognized that one of the men had pinned his trouser leg, allowing him to make no progress at all.

"My, my, my; lookie here what we got!"

"Hold! Listen, I probably knew your very father."

They were taking it in the greatest merriment; he remembered his indignation that they could look so lightly upon a murdering man.

"Let's go downtown, you want to?"

"No."

"Let's do."

He found himself being hustled downstairs at far greater speed than he liked. A tiny crowd had gathered, some dozen of persons, all of them grinning the grin that has ever accompanied the condemned to the stake. The car itself was plush and warm but smelled of hair oil, shoe polish, and snuff. The radio apparatus was infinitely more complex than in '49 and '47—this one had knobs and buttons and warning lights. Yet the voice was just as hoarse and came in the same amputated spurts as when he had been a nine-year-old in the clutches for the first time of these people's grandfather-police.

He tried to enjoy it; he had to assume this was simply their strategy for earning a living, even if they could just as well have read about it instead. The town itself was full of Christmas shoppers—enviable people, red-cheeked . . . He was close to weeping. It seemed to him monstrous how little they knew about his *quality*, in fact nothing, and never would. He sat, looking straight ahead with that dignity that belongs to people who choose not to resist. His soul, of course, *that* was free, and not so much running behind as hovering overhead. Now that he really was captured and pressed in between two gross organisms (compacted, as it seemed to him, not from ligament and bone, but lymph, pure and simple), he began to consider what might happen. Not much. They might snatch his life away—he didn't want it. Indeed, he could picture himself bidding farewell very happily, even to taking out his kerchief and waving with it. Or, they might keep him squeezed in between two bodies full with gas, in which event he would simply abandon to them his body and fly off with his soul! How well he knew them! They had been granted every chance to develop and had always refused to do so. Then too, if he could not by some stratagem or another break out of this circle of weak minds, then did he merit any cruelty that weak minds could invent.

The journey needed twenty minutes. At one moment he had taken out his matches and was using them when the man slapped them out of his hand. Lee looked at him. He still could not specify what it was precisely about these late twentieth-century faces, whether atrophy or entropy, anomie or satiety. This one had corruption to the lids; Lee did not want the man's exudations on him. Moreover, whereas ignorant people in the past might have been unwashed, or have had ear and nose clogged clown-wise in hair, this man was entirely glabrous, no doubt a portent of the future when pus and corruption afforded nothing to grow roots in. Lee came closer.

"What the hell you looking at?"

"You ever read Ortega y Gasset?"

"Fuck you."

"No, you should! Or heck, you could start by reading some of those books that used to be mine."

Useless, the man had gone back to picking his teeth. Looking at him, Lee could remember the very moment, years ago, when he had broken with common man.

"Tell me, how's your football team doing this year?"

"I tell you what, we could stop and take care of you right here and now. Is that what you want?"

"No."

"Then shut up."

He had expected the same merry secretary who used to wear such memorable sweaters; instead, there was a computer in the corner. He had no slightest doubt but that he was soon to be attached to the thing and analyzed. Formerly, he could cry his way out of prison, but not now, not with the machine taking down everything he said.

They put him in a chair then stepped back, the two of them, to get a better look. The wall-eyed man had the authority; it was the young one that worried Lee.

"Just like to know why it is, *Sir*, that you don't pay your rent?"

"What's that?"

"Rent. Don't believe Mrs. DeBardeleben much appreciates you running off like that without paying your rent."

Tea room rent! Lee smiled.

"And how about that little boy?"

"Oh for God's sake. You're not going to tell me I *murdered* someone!"

"We hadn't had no murders. Why, did *you* murder somebody?"

"Apparently not."

"That little boy—you *meant* to murder him. Didn't you?"

"Oh for God's sake. Look, if you knew what he was like . . ."

"You have any idea who his daddy is? Huh?"

"Oh for God's sake. I didn't have access to the daddy!" Useless. Suddenly, he stood. "I need to piss."

"Well don't do it here."

He was taken down the hall to a narrow closet with toilet. There *was* a window. It *was* cracked open a bit; however, he looked upon it as a trap. His first scheme was to refuse to come out; his second, that if he but concentrated with his will, the man might turn and involuntarily drift away. Somewhere a telephone was ringing.

He got one foot out and then, his joy increasing by leaps, followed it up with a leg. He had grown so thin that he could throw out his limbs one by one and make a pile of them in the grass. It came to him that this was one of the finest things he had ever done, that it was unbelievable, daring, and impossibly good, and that out of all of history it had been reserved for *him* to do it.

There was a yard and no one watching; he was able to walk across and then, taking his courage, back into *the same building whence he had left.* Worst was the slowness, the length of the hall, the door; finally, he was outside again. He had one minute exactly for a new piece of grand luck to come his way. Behind him the station had not yet exploded, though he waited for it from one heartbeat to the next.

His luck came in the form of a little black taxi waiting there all these years.

Twenty-one

THE DRIVER WAS A JOCUND MAN, A talker too. Lee let him go on at length, all the way down to the woods, then paid him off in such good bills as that he would never wish to report about it. The line of trees had shrunk back a few inches since his day, the lower foliage especially, where a certain late twentieth-century etiolation had taken hold. Nevertheless, he stepped quickly and was thirty feet deep into the woods before night began to fall. The music of the crickets! He had to laugh out loud. By any measure they were supposed to be hibernating by now.

He might have tarried here a week, but for lack of sleeping facilities. Then too, he had lost his ancient ability of walking noiselessly in leaves. *And* he had no cane.

An hour later and he was in deep, so deep that even if he turned back now he was likely to miss the town in the dark. True, the radio tower was still to be seen: the topmost lantern had turned a flashing blue in token of his escape. It gave him great pleasure.

It was a very black night, with black trees and birds brushing so close as to make a personal affront of it. Twice he lashed out, not with cane but a branch of near size. Something was astir—now he saw it, a transparent glass lizard with organs all in view. Usually, he knew, the truth came as a great shock, whereas *nothing* surprised him anymore; nature was in decay.

He came up over a hill, half-expecting, as it were, a new-age ocean, pink and silent; instead, it was a woldland all in shadow. When he died it must be from beauty, the kind that would have him shaking his head and wringing his hands while leaving him weaker each time. Further, his patience was running out. He wanted beauty from both barrels, full in the face and no longer merely teasing about the edges. Suddenly, that moment, the moon contracted violently, darkened, then came back on in X rays. For one brief moment, he was vouchsafed a vision of the thing in all its hollowness and the tremendous number of souls inside required for all time to roll large-sized balls of dung about.

Midnight discovered him counting his money under a tree. By his estimate, he was a full seven miles into the forest, and it was many more miles before the next settlement. There were hills behind, smoke coming off the summits. He seemed to remember an orchard in this vicinity, with mule and press for squeezing; now, knowing what he knew, the mule had disappeared and the cider had all long ago been consumed. He had great pity for himself, an old man always handled unfairly—not for the life of him could he say how he had come to such a pass. The last he remembered he was young and of a unique arrogance, and even now he would have preferred it that way. He lit a cigarette; then he again started in on that high-pitched moaning that sounded ludicrous even in his own ear.

She came to him in dark clothing, noiseless and young. One moment he was squinting into the trees; the next, there were two calm familiar brown eyes on a level with his own.

"I have no place to live in!"

"I know."

"And very little money too!"

"I know, I know." (She was standing on his knee, four inches tall.) "But soon you'll not have to worry about that."

"How do you figure?"

"Well! Let's not forget you're seventy-three years old. And then too, it's going to be very cold tonight."

"Cold?"

"*Very* cold."

"Ah."

"See what I mean?"

"Ah ha!"

"See?

"Yes! Yes, I *do* see!"

He stood at once, took off his coat and walked away from it. The money was no use, and yet, he found himself against his own best will and determination coming back for it after all. Another ingenious idea came to mind—to take off his shirts as well.

He had wanted his death by heat, being too old to experience cold in its full meaning. Too old, too thin, his head too occupied with books. He *was* amused at the spectacle, all the more so that he had taken recently to using suspenders. He was quite cheerful. He made a mental note: "There was no fear."

* * *

Sometimes he went forward, sometimes he slept. One time he heard his dog yapping to come out and play. These phenomena were strange—never would he have expected *vomiting* from the result of cold.

He had come far. He saw what he thought to be a hamlet; in fact, they were the distant spires and steeples of the egregious Birmingham itself. Yet he could not honestly say that he was not dreaming. His one great dread was that the sun with its famous warmth might come and bring him back to earth again.